TITLE II - A

A CASTLE
OF BONE

PENELOPE FARMER

A CASTLE
OF BONE

A Margaret K. McElderry Book

ATHENEUM *NEW YORK*

1973

J
F

For Judy
with love,
and for
Sandy Hayhurst
who made writing
this book possible

A CASTLE
OF BONE

... And bones of solidness froze
Over all his nerves of joy ...

WILLIAM BLAKE

The achievement of Manwyddan the wise
After lamentation and fiery wrath
Was a construction of the bone fortress of Oeth and Anoeth.

WELSH TRIAD

CHAPTER 1

"WHAT's that noise?" asked Jean. They all stood staring at the cupboard. Penn against the light looked huge – his hair edged by light, blazed, caught sun, almost reflected it.

"What noise?" Penn asked.

"But there's nothing," Hugh said, "except my wallet." Penn's sister Anna had just put it there, then closed the cupboard door.

"Oh wait, oh *listen*," timid Anna said.

And there was a noise; very small at first; rustlings, tappings, scrapings – but gradually louder, like a tree Hugh thought, a tree growing inside the cupboard, its branches dragging, rapping against the door, blown by some hidden wind. In a moment the sound, increasing, was of neither tree nor wind: it was a huge sound booming within those narrow wooden walls, some huge form banging and racketing in there. And he heard another sound also, as loud as the first, but tighter, shriller, which sounded, only it could not be, like the squealing of a pig.

Penn as usual took Hugh's decision for him; leaned forward, pulled open both the cupboard doors. Within the instant of the click a large white sow fell out, rolled over, picked itself up and blundered, terrified, across the room – quite unmistakably a real pig, with hanging dugs and crude, prehistoric-looking skin. Hugh, though dazed, could see the little bristles that edged its ears, saw the blue symbol stamped on its flank, like the price mark stamped on supermarket goods, as it missed Anna by inches, knocked over his cluttered chair —

7

"Hugh, the *door*, watch out," Penn yelled, too late, because the pig which had not for one moment ceased to squeal, dashed through, turned sideways and fell down the first and narrowest flight of stairs. Hugh, diving to Penn's shout, was unable to check the movement of his hand, slammed the door shut, and as he opened it again the pig fell down more stairs, crashed with full bulk, dangerously, against quivering bannisters, careered along the landing, down a third flight, thundered its feet on the wooden hall floor then shot out of the door into the front garden, Penn and the others in confused pursuit.

Hugh saw Jean's cat bolt upright on a flowerbed watching them; he saw the pig now lurching but still swift enough, run out through the open garden gate. Jean was wailing like a little girl.

"It'll get run over, it'll get run over."

"We'd better try heading it to the park," shrieked Penn.

The gate crashed shut behind them with a clash of iron. The wooden fence shivered all along its length. The black cat watching had not shifted fractionally.

"Your ma must have heard," Penn was saying breathlessly to Hugh.

"She might not. I think she's out. Jesus, just look at it" – he saw the pig weave erratically across the road – "something's going to hit it *soon*."

"At least they slow down here – but on the main road..." Penn took speed again. Ahead of him the pig took speed too, its tail uncurled by speed streaming out behind, and by good luck turned right (the way they needed if they were to drive it towards the park), first kept to the pavement for twenty yards or so, then swerved diagonally towards the traffic island in the middle of the road, where at last it paused. Perhaps the blink of the orange beacons had bewildered it. A

8

car almost halted at the crossing too; thought better of it, jerked on; the pig as immediately decided to move. Pig squeal met brake squeal. Whether pig actually met car was impossible to tell, but its flight continued more furiously than ever, while everywhere along the road people stopped and turned and heads shot from cars. Anna and Jean slowed, panting. Hugh entangled himself with a woman and a yellow dog. Even Penn was not close enough to head the pig up the first road leading to the park, and would have failed at the second probably, had not the pig itself swerved wildly and taken that road of its own accord.

There was a gate at the far end. It was designed to keep deer from getting out of the park, so might not normally have let in a pig, only a man happened to be holding it open for a woman with a pram. Neither noticed the pig until it careered past them; at which the startled man let the gate swing back, barring the pig's exit to the road, but leaving its entrance clear into the park. It ran itself once, frantically, into the iron bars. The second time freely, easily, it ran out, through the trees towards a patch of summer bracken. White pig, they saw, black trees, green bracken. Then the pig vanished. They did not see it any more. Almost at once they ceased to hear it squeal.

CHAPTER 2

IT had taken Hugh and his father most of the morning to find
that cupboard. Hugh's room had sloping corners and a
window looking into the ash tree, but till now it had had no
cupboard, and in one of her periodic domestic agitations his
mother had declared that he needed one and sent them both
out to look. Hugh, having better things to do with a Saturday at the beginning of the summer holidays, argued that he
had hung his clothes on hooks for years, so what, suddenly,
was wrong with hooks now? And if he must have a cupboard, why did he, Hugh, have to help look for it? A cupboard was a cupboard was a cupboard. He did not mind
what it looked like. His father said that hooks were adequate
but cupboards better; that Hugh with his artistic pretensions
should know better than anyone that function should not be
divorced from appearance, and if he did not know this was
it not about time he learnt? Furthermore, he said, jamming
on the battered green felt hat that he wore regardless, both
winter and summer, he was not basically interested in buying
a cupboard for Hugh either, a fact Hugh would never have
guessed from the amount of unlikely and unsuitable shops he
seemed prepared to explore in search of it.

They had found themselves at last, both hot and cross and
bored, outside a junk shop in a little street that ran down
towards the river. There was a trestle table on the pavement
with a heap of old music sheets on it, torn and dog-eared,
another heap of scratched 78-speed records, a tray of
battered, shineless jewellery, chipped plates, chipped cups
stacked precariously, also a cardboard box which said 6X20

Country Vegetable in two inch high blue letters and held an assortment of bleached and dusty books. ANTIQUES the board above the door said. "Junk," shouted Hugh's father, striding under the board and into the shop, turning impatiently to beckon Hugh after him.

Inside Hugh sneezed twice, rapidly. It was at least as radical a change of environment as would have been plunging under the sea. Every sense shocked, retreated, reorganised itself. His skin, at chill, produced goose pimples, his nose sneezed at dust and mould and damp and another, sweeter, but as aged smell, and his eyes seemed to fade in the dim, furred, almost tangible light. To his ears the sounds that escaped from the outside world seemed distorted, like sounds at the far end of a narrow tunnel.

Never in his life had he seen so many things crammed into so small a space – furniture piled up, pictures fitted together on the walls without an inch between them, every table and chair heaped with smaller objects, spoons and ornaments and candlesticks, fans and necklaces, inkwells and ash trays, books and more records. Even the ceiling was crowded, hung with chairs and tables like angular creepers, among which Hugh's father had to duck his head. The shop altogether was like a forest, Hugh thought, a close dark jungle. But a forest without life; nothing moved in it. For a moment with a shock Hugh saw a white face watching them, but it was a china face on a china head, with blind white eyes and a pale, straw-like wig.

There was a gramophone as well as records. Hugh would not have recognised the rectangular black box, but his father did. Snatching a record from the pile and setting it on the green baize turntable, he fitted a handle into a slot and wound up the gramophone. As the turntable spun round, scratchy but lively music began to jitter across the shop.

The old man stood between a low cupboard and a tall chair watching them. They did not see him come, nor where he had come from. There were gaps between objects, here and there, but nothing as defined as a doorway, though there must have been some way into the back of the shop, Hugh thought.

"We're looking for a cupboard," he shouted guiltily above the music, for his father, jigging to it rapturously, still seemed to have noticed nothing. "That cupboard," he said pointing. His eyes fleeing beyond the old man, he had noticed the cupboard for the first time.

The old man had come nearer then and taken off the needle arm and stopped the gramophone. The music left a shadow of itself, then was altogether gone. Yet it was still to that, to the sound of something called Dinah's Ragtime Boogie – conjuring from some unexpected corner of his memory irrelevant images of feathered and beaded ladies jigging rhythmically among potted palms – that Hugh saw it – his cupboard – for the first time.

Immediately he had never in his life wanted anything as much as he wanted that, not even his first box of proper oil paints.

It was extraordinary that he could have wanted the cupboard so much. "It's monstrous, abominable," his father said. And Hugh could not have denied it if he tried. Yet that had not made any difference to him. And his father was so bored with the search by now that he did not bother to argue the point for long. At least it was a cupboard and cheap at that. A cupboard he had, after all, been instructed to find.

CHAPTER 3

THE houses were joined, a pair, tall, pointed and curious; either unsymmetric without the other. Their windows had stonework like eyebrows over them. Along this road all the houses were in pairs, but no pair was like any other one, the gables different, in particular, some as curvilinear and plump as in this pair they were angular and sharp. The right-hand house had recently been converted, and Penn and Anna's parents had bought the flat made of the top two floors. All the paint on this house was new, builders' sand and ladders still littering the garden at the front of it. But Hugh's and Jean's parents had lived in the whole of the left-hand house as long as Jean at least could remember, and it had not been painted for easily as long as that. The paint was a faded pink, the stonework yellowish. Rhubarb and custard Penn called it when he wanted to annoy Hugh.

The cupboard arrived there that evening, long after Hugh had given up hope of it. The sun – a fire between crimson and scarlet – squatted on the skyline as they carried it in through the garden gate; two men in stained white aprons, oily-headed, who mopped themselves and complained bitterly, in dualogue, when it came to lugging the thing up three flights of Victorian stairs. How in all the supernatural . . . could it be so heavy they wondered, and indeed Hugh wondered too, for as cupboards go it did not look particularly heavy. Its doors, swung open, looked thin as match-board.

"Shoddy, there you are, Hugh, I told you so," declared his father with gloomy satisfaction. "Ain't known another like it, for weight not," the balder of the two men said as he closed his fingers round Hugh's father's inevitably flamboyant tip.

"It's hideous, monstrous," Hugh's father said with enjoyment, examining the cupboard carefully again.

But when Hugh went to bed that night, his clothes were still strewn about the room. He did not know what had stopped him putting them away in the cupboard. Not laziness certainly, though he was usually lazy about such things. But some odd reluctance that he did not try to explain.

And in bed, when he shut his eyes, the empty cupboard assumed . . . in the darkness . . . What it assumed did not frighten, so much as exhilarate, him; his heart thumped extraordinarily. Yet he would not let himself analyse what he felt. He forced his mind away into pictures, images.

He began to try to visualise the cupboard. He had tried before, that morning after they had bought it. His father had decided to have a drink and Hugh had sat on the wall overlooking the river with a glass of Coca-cola beside him, trying to remember what the cupboard looked like.

But he had not been able to. If momentarily he had caught some detail, immediately he had attempted to fit another to it, it would slide away again. He had had a very strong feeling of it, yet could not translate this visually, which had annoyed him because as a rule he was not only observant, but practised consciously retaining what he observed, in order to use it in his painting. He had come to do this almost automatically. Yet now in bed, though he had seen the cupboard once again, when he tried to visualise it, still no picture came into his mind.

Instead he saw other images from that morning beside the river: the Coca-Cola – a dark elliptical liquid in the glass with a small white moon in it of reflected light. When he had raised his eyes from that, there had been across the river a group of trees, and now in bed that image crowded out the nearer one. They were a group of willows and alders, the alders darker, dourer-looking than the pollarded willow trees.

The group seemed to be closing in on him, rushing towards him through his head. In a moment he could focus on one tree only, in a moment more could see only an area of trunk quite close to him. He reached out a hand, involuntarily. He touched wood. His fingers scraped on, scraped up, wood bark. He opened his eyes. He was standing among alder trees, facing one trunk, one tree. When he took his hand away from it, there was green from the bark beneath his fingernails.

The trees that morning, which had stood in line, now encircled him, and there were no willows, only alder trees. There was a fire, too, in the middle of the grove, burning fiercely, with hints of blue and green flame. A girl sat by the fire, feeding it big and little sticks. Hugh could not see her face because her head was bent away from him, but she had very black, very straight, hair and a red dress and bare white feet.

He realised that he himself was still wearing pyjamas. Seeing the girl, he clutched the jacket about him, for it was flapping open, having lost all but one of its buttons. (He had told his mother about the buttons, several times. "Oh, I'll sew them on for you, love," she had said each time, but the jacket had always come back from being washed, neatly folded but still buttonless. Jean would have sewed them on, if he had asked, but Hugh had never remembered to ask her.)

The girl made no move. She did not look at Hugh. He was not even sure that she had noticed him. The river ran beyond the alder grove, and on the other side of it, near the bridge, a man stood fishing. Beyond the river was the hill.

There was no town now. The hill was bare except for a few trees, and on top of it a square and turreted castle. The falling sun caught one side fleetingly and made the turrets look as if they had been painted red.

The instant Hugh saw this castle he knew he had to reach it. He began to move but meanwhile the girl poked at the fire so violently that it glared for a moment with brilliant light, with particularly bright and fiery heat, and the heat felt like a wall through which he had to break. It receded behind him afterwards. Immediately he pulled himself through what felt like another wall – of what he did not know, only that it was hostile to him – and so passed out of the ring of alder trees.

He did not look at the girl again. He had never properly seen her face, but the way she had moved stirred some memory in him, which was as quickly gone.

He crossed the river then by the bridge, not the arched stone bridge that he knew, but a flat wooden one, standing on wooden piles driven into the river-bed. Though broad enough to take a cart or chariot it had no sides to it. It felt curiously comfortable and warm to Hugh's bare feet, as if it was alive, with warm blood in it.

The sun was vanishing behind the hill. Clutching his jacket round him, Hugh went on through chillier air and fading light, thorns and stones attacking his feet, his legs beginning to ache. He could not see the castle any more. It might have been the slope which hid his view, it might have been the growing darkness. He went on anyway, climbing steeply now.

CHAPTER 4

THE next morning, Sunday, Hugh's mother at breakfast pointed out what dirty nails he had.

"They're green, Hugh. They're disgusting. Whatever have you been doing?"

Hugh thought: I had green nails in my dream.

His mother did not often notice such things. But when she did it was with a vehemence that made him immediately rebellious, even about things to which he was usually indifferent. He and his mother were like two loose ends of charged wire these days, for touched together they sparked dramatically. So now, he rushed from the kitchen, shouting, and ran upstairs as noisily as he could, slamming the bathroom door on his way past.

The noise chastened him a little. He flung himself down on his bed with a feeling of anti-climax, regretting his half-eaten and now unobtainable breakfast. Almost immediately he picked himself up and went down to the bathroom on the half-landing and scrubbed his nails clean. By the time he started back upstairs to his room, he was feeling perfectly calm, though the tips of his fingers were smarting.

It was at the third step up that he began to have a most odd sensation. He had been thinking about the cupboard, waiting empty in his room. And suddenly it was as if the idea of it had gone outside his mind; it was as if it was pulling him from his room, while at the same time something else tried to drag him back. This something Hugh recognised after a moment as his own alarm, making him resist the pull ahead, as the gravity of an object makes it resist the contrary pull of

17

a magnet, until he recognised what it was; then, fear lessening, the pull became irresistible and he went on up and in. To find what? Nothing as far as he could tell that was not entirely ordinary. The sun had sought out and lit the cupboard making it look cheaper, more featureless than ever. A bird shifted in the ash tree outside the window. In order to create some movement, anything, to release and justify the tension he had felt, Hugh picked up a shirt and flung it on his unmade bed.

Shortly afterwards Penn arrived to see Hugh, and with him Anna to see Jean. All of them drifted into Hugh's room to look at the new cupboard.

"It's not much to look at, is it though?" Jean had said.

The pig emerged from the cupboard not long afterwards.

When the pig had finally disappeared, they continued walking through the park. No one suggested it – no one at first said anything. They had just looked at each other and walked on, over rough grass and reddish, stony paths. Even Penn had lost his ebullience, and Jean did not attempt her usual underrunning commentary of sensible suggestions and sensible explanations. They were all stunned; partly by fear, not so much of the pig itself, but of its inexplicable appearance; partly by simple astonishment. They were much more frightened now than previously because at first there had been no time for fear.

"What would we have done with it if we had caught it?" Penn said at last. "Perhaps it's just as well we didn't."

"We couldn't possibly have caught it," Jean said.

They were walking on open ground just here, at almost the highest point of the park. Two men were trying to fly kites – South American bird kites – scarlet, widespread, magnificent. But there was scarcely enough wind, the birds tugged up occasionally as if about to soar, then more often dipped, fluttered, dived back to earth.

"As if they were wounded," Anna said. They went through a gate into the plantation. There was a stream there and water plants, rushes and irises and orange flags, and trees, birch trees mostly, dappled, insubstantial-looking, some black and white, others with bark as satiny and wood as rough, but with a russet, even purplish sheen on them; trees like snake skin, Hugh thought.

"Like giraffe's legs," Anna said.

"Whatever are you talking about?" Penn asked.

"Enormously tall giraffes," said Hugh.

"They mean the birch trees, I think," said Jean.

"Don't be an idiot, Ann," Penn spoke with such scorn that Hugh came in to rescue Anna, though it was impossible to tell from her face whether she needed rescuing or not.

"What do you think happened, Penn? That pig, I mean."

"I can't believe it did happen. It's impossible," said Penn.

"But it did; we know it did," said Jean.

"Of course I know it happened. I never said it didn't. I just said it seems impossible. There must be some logical explanation. There always is a logical reason if you look hard enough. You'd think a car impossible if you didn't look inside at the engine."

"Clever Penn," said Jean, a mixture of admiration and sarcasm in her voice. Perhaps, just, admiration more.

"It could have been magic," Anna said.

"Oh, *Ann*. I *said*. There must be some logical explanation."

"Well, how else did a pig appear in an empty cupboard?" asked Jean.

"We all saw it was empty," added Hugh.

"It could have come upstairs . . ." But even Penn knew that it had not. "It could have come in at the door," he suggested defiantly. "Who was looking at the door? No one was."

"Oh come off it," said Hugh. "A thing that size. And you heard what a racket it made afterwards."

"Magic," said Anna, looking obstinate. Hugh had never known her speak as much as she had today. Normally she never said anything, not when he was around anyway, and she looked timid, even terrified; she appeared the opposite of Penn, negative to his positive, a small shadow beside his large sun.

"Well I don't believe in magic," Jean said.

"Not like some," interrupted Penn.

"But I just don't see how else . . ."

"Suppose it was just a hallucination after all."

"Suppose we imagined it. Suppose it never really happened."

Hugh, looking round him now, could almost have believed Penn, almost wanted to believe him. They had reached a space of emerald grass fringed by more silver birches and rowan trees. The grass was too green, too soft, too smooth; the rowan berries scarlet, the tree trunks speckled black and white. It looked as unreal as elfland, Hugh thought, a place to which men were enticed in fairy tales and from which they never returned – like Sir Orfeo, or Thomas the Rhymer – except that both those had returned at last.

There were other people here and a dog or two, walking across the grass; but they dissolved into the landscape, they seemed no more real than it. Not even time seemed real any more to Hugh. Thomas and Sir Orfeo had left time as well as space when they went to fairyland, and now he and Penn and Jean and Anna were outside time too because what had happened could not belong to time, which was reality, or the reality they understood. The pig must be a hallucination. It had to be.

But even as he thought that, Hugh remembered it; its bulk, its thunderous careering, the smell and sound of it, the bristles on its skin. This place might seem unreal, but nothing could have looked more real than the pig, or been more real.

"Oh come off it, Penn. It was real all right. Anyway four people don't have the same hallucination all at once."

"Okay. Let's say it was real then." Penn bent down, picked up a birch twig, folded back his body and with it his right arm, and hurled with perfect ease and rhythm. They saw the twig arc, collide with other trees, pass among their branches with uneven percussive sounds, then fall, losing momentum, to meet ground at last. The flickering leaves of birch, like Penn's flickering red gold hair, gave an illusion of light, though the sun had disappeared.

Anna, Hugh noticed, intently watched Penn throw. When he had finished Penn glanced at her, but by then, hastily, she had looked away.

Anna's face took on an odd misshapen look as they were walking towards home again. Penn, noticing, told her sharply to stop chewing her tongue. It made her look even more hideous than usual, he said.

Jean said, "Oh that's what she's doing, is it? I've often wondered."

"She's always doing it. It makes Mum wild, you can see why."

"It helps me think, that's all," Anna said. She dropped behind them and walked along the path alone. Hugh could not forget her at his back. She felt a weight on his heels, a load, almost oppressing him. He thought that was because he felt sorry for her, Penn having been so fierce, and at last he too held back to let her catch him up. Penn and Jean went on a little ahead of them, Penn flicking neatly at grasses with a stick.

"What were you thinking, Anna?" Hugh asked.

Anna did not reply.

"Anything might help. Anything you thought of – however unlikely. Everything seems unlikely now."

"Your wallet, the one I put in the cupboard. What was it made of?"

"Why did you put it in the cupboard, Anna? A wallet, of all things . . ."

"I don't know. Why shouldn't I put something in. It was empty, the cupboard," Anna said. When Hugh looked at her he could not see her face at all. Her head was bent. Her dark hair swung down.

His wallet was so old and familiar he had scarcely looked at it for years. To remember it properly he had to think quite hard. Inside and out it had been a pale, pinkish colour, darkened in some places more than others by both age and dirt. Its edges had been whipped with a narrow thong.

"Leather," he said.

"And leather is . . ."

"Skin, of course," Penn turned, overhearing them.

"Anna wondered what my wallet was."

"What sort of skin?" Anna asked.

"Horse skin, cow skin, sheep skin," Penn said.

"Deer skin," Hugh said. They had left the park by now and were passing a pub called The Roebuck. A roedeer leapt across the faded sign.

"What about your wallet anyway?" asked Jean.

"Well, Anna put it in the cupboard and the next thing was the pig came out."

"That doesn't mean your wallet had anything to do with it."

"What sort of leather was it?" insisted Anna, obstinately.

"I don't know," Hugh said. "It's so old. It was Dad's first, then mine."

"We'll have a look when we get back," said Penn. "But I don't suppose it's relevant."

But the cupboard was empty. They thought the pig in its rush must have knocked the wallet out. They hunted everywhere for it, peering under chairs, under the bed, crawling on hands and knees. But they could not find it.

"It would be easier, Hugh, if your room was tidier," Jean said. "Now you've got the cupboard why don't you put your clothes away?"

"I don't suppose it's relevant, anyway," said Penn.

They went their separate ways. Hugh had a contented, solitary afternoon. Until the evening he almost forgot about the cupboard. Certainly, though he was painting, his easel set up next to it, he did not feel the presence of it at all.

In the evening he sat on the edge of his bed wearing his slippers and his pyjamas. His knees jutted uncomfortably – the bed was low and his legs of late seemed to have grown inconveniently long. He had raised his hand and put it to the lamp, the image of which hung infinitesimally behind his eyes after he had extinguished it. He did not at once take his hand from the switch.

For in the darkness, he felt again what he had felt on the stairs that morning; the pulling forward and dragging back, attraction, repulsion, simultaneously. But now both impulses seemed to be inside his head and they drew him to, drew him from – what?

Hugh remembered last night; the image of his Coca-Cola glass displaced by the alder grove. Tonight was different though, because he realised he had been expecting something similar to happen, whereas last night he had been expecting nothing. He also had the feeling that he ought to be able to control it, or at least to decide whether it happened or not. But he could only control anything to the extent that he could control himself – or rather his own mind – and how could he do that, he thought, rather resentfully, when he did not even know what his area of decision was. He let his will go anyway, with scarcely a struggle; opened his mind, grabbed a picture out of air, to have it displaced at once by trees, maddening trees, that melted from light to dark, from visibility to invisibility; birch trees, naturally.

He stood at the edge of a wood, at night, with above a silver moon and stars, and on the ground a scattering of snow. The leaf mould beneath the snow had a film of frost on it. Layers cracked lightly when he moved his feet – it was a sensation rather than a sound which made him glad he wore slippers as well as his pyjamas, though both seemed inadequate, not to say ridiculous, for such a time and place. Fortunately Jean had yesterday sewn his buttons on, so he was able at least to do the jacket up.

He was quite alone this time. He looked back almost hopefully into the birch wood in case the girl was there. But he saw only moon-made lights and shadows that looked as bright and as dark, alternately, as the trunks of the trees themselves.

Ahead was a bare and empty country, oddly magnified, in sweeps and hollows, with what might have been a track but masked by snow. In the distance as he expected, stood the castle, and he stepped out towards it knowing that he must. But he stopped almost at once, abruptly; first startled, then for a moment terrified.

There was something black lying in the snow. He had noticed it, but not taken in what it was since it lay motionless, well to the right of the direction he had to take. But now from the corner of an eye he saw it move, and as he swung round towards it, heard an uncanny cry that left him tight with fear. The black thing divided. Part wheeled up and rode away, calling, on the air – a crow, Hugh thought. It made other cruel and unearthly sounds. But at least he recognised what it was.

Reluctantly he altered his path a little and went towards the black thing that remained behind.

It was another crow, but dead. Black feathers lay on the white snow and drops of fresh blood. Red blood, thought Hugh, though the moonlight had bleached the colour out. He thought of the black-haired girl in the red dress with a strange nostalgic kind of ache, feeling suddenly lonelier than in all his life before.

He shook himself. He went on, alone, towards the castle. It looked almost transparent tonight, it might have been made of glass or ice. In places the walls were so white, so staring, they were like mirrors reflecting moonlight, while elsewhere they were so black it was as if Hugh looked right through them to the night sky itself. There were even little points of light upon the black that could have been the stars.

He seemed to see patterns spiralling up the turrets nearest him; or they could have been staircases mounting within transparent walls; but no matter how much he strained his eyes, he could not have said for certain which.

The moon had come to seem particular, like a lamp to guide a traveller to the castle.

On went Hugh, stumbling over rough ground with tufts of grass that tipped and emptied snow into his bedroom slippers, having to pick his way so carefully that he took his eyes from the castle ahead of him. Meanwhile clouds crept up, unnoticed, to engulf the moon. It rode among them visibly at first, though dimmed. Then it was altogether gone. When Hugh looked up again he could not see the castle any more.

He could not see anything. Not only the castle had gone but the wood behind him. The wind had risen – winds drove around Hugh, needled and bit him, rent and buffeted. Snow seemed to whirl at him from all the corners of the world. Then he shut his eyes and there was only dark. He felt his knees humped up, his feet jammed hard against the floor. They were icy and his slippers sopping wet. He took his hand from the electric switch, toppled into bed, dragged his blankets round him and slept all night, exhausted, and with wet slippers on.

CHAPTER 5

HUGH and Penn were in some ways the most unlikely friends; their living next door to each other mere chance, irrelevant to the fact that they were friends. They did not even go to the same school, and out of school their interests were entirely different. Hugh read, dreamed, gazed out of the window, and drew continually when he was not actually painting. Penn chiefly played games. He belonged to most school teams and played in scratch teams during the holidays. The rest of the time he and Hugh were inseparable, more or less.

He went to the local grammar school, Hugh to a private school, but both were in continual trouble for doing little there, other than what they liked doing anyway. Thus they kept each other company at the bottom of their mediocre classes (at Hugh's school, politely, his was called Remove) though Penn did maintain even this position rather more easily, while Hugh was threatened periodically with still further demotion to a class whose master he disliked heartily and so had to undertake furious, if short-lived, bouts of formal work.

Hugh envied mildly Penn's not needing to do the same. He was irritated occasionally by Penn's admonitions to him to buck up, pull his socks up, stir his stumps and the like. Mostly, though, he scarcely even noticed them, let the bossiness float away, evaporate.

For, much more, Hugh liked Penn's certainties. Things got started and done without his bothering to have to make up his own mind; which did not stop him exploring

mentally his own rather different plans and ideas, only meant
he need not risk spoiling them by putting them into action
too soon or in the wrong way, so destroying patterns that he
felt himself on the verge of discovering. Moreover it suited
him to be left alone so much to paint while Penn was
occupied with playing games.

He did not feel either superior or inferior to Penn, except
in respects he did not care about. He just felt different, that
was all. And he enjoyed sitting in the light of the sun that
Penn represented to the world, because then people, dazzled,
did not notice him. He could have done with having Penn to
protect him at school too.

What Penn saw in Hugh was much less obvious.

That morning, Monday, Penn came round after breakfast;
after his breakfast, that is. (Being the holidays, Hugh and
Jean's mother got theirs in what she called her own time,
which meant late, unless they came down and got it first.)
He clattered down the stairs to the basement looking too tall
for the ceiling, though he was not – Hugh was taller, and
even he did not have to bend his head. Anna trailed after,
looking tired and pale, in a rather short black cotton dress.
She tended to wear clothes like that, which her mother
chose and liked and which suited *her*, but which did not suit,
indeed often eclipsed, Anna.

"Coffee, Penn?" Hugh's mother asked vaguely, from
behind a newspaper, nibbling as if accidentally at her third
slice of toast.

"I don't like coffee much."

"Milk? Help yourself. Or toast."

"No thanks, I won't." Penn looked at Hugh very pointedly. "Are you nearly ready, Hugh? We've got an awful lot
to talk about."

The arguments, however, had not altered since the day

before, so that Jean, left downstairs for a while to help wash
up, did not miss anything. Anna protested magic twice in a
small voice, then stood by the window, gazing out, existing
on the fringes of the room and of the argument. Penn was, if
anything, more insistent than ever on some logical ordinary
explanation for what had happened, and Hugh himself
would have preferred to believe Penn today. For he had
picked up one of his slippers to find it not only damp still but
water-stained and with a small, dead birch leaf stuck to the
crinkled rubber sole. As he could not for the life of him
remember how or why this could be so, the implications
both puzzled and disturbed him.

August had asserted itself after the greyness of the day
before. The sun poured into Hugh's room generously,
openly, and by its light the cupboard could not have
appeared more commonplace and shoddy. It had been so
thickly varnished that even the natural grain of the wood
appeared artificial, with one door at least as golden and shiny
as syrup. The other was only a little darker. "It must have
had a mirror on it once," said Penn. "You can see the screw
holes."

"And the glue," Hugh added; there was a trace of glue in
the moulding at the top.

Inside the cupboard was no less ordinary, though less
objectionable to look at, even pleasant. The wood, unvarn-
ished, actually looked like wood, paler, pinker, and without
a gloss. On the left was a row of shelves and on the right
three curly brass hooks jutted above their heads. A thin brass
rail ran across the top of the cupboard. There was another,
thinner rail on the door for ties.

"What is it? What's it made of?" Penn asked.

"What do you think. Raffia?"

"No, platinum actually," Penn said, sarcastically.

"Gold would be prettier. Not that this is exactly pretty."

"Platinum's more valuable. I meant what *wood*, fool, idiot."

"*I* don't know," said Hugh.

"I thought you did carpentry?"

"New wood's different, it's white; well, yellowish."

"What sort of wood might you use to make a cupboard?"

"Mahogany, pine, oak . . ."

"Well, which is this then?"

"It doesn't look like any of them to me. Mahogany's redder, oak's darker and much coarser-grained. I don't know otherwise. There are lots of strange African woods they use now. It could be anything."

Penn went over to the window then. Anna, very deliberately, moved away. "Could it be ash?" he asked, gazing out.

"Not possibly; it's the wrong colour. They make boats from ash, mostly anyway. It doesn't try to spring straight when you curve it, which is good for the ribs of boats."

"Gawd, aren't we knowledgeable," said Penn.

"So, what about it?" asked Hugh.

"It's a fat lot of use when you can't even tell what sort of wood this cupboard is."

Hugh went to Penn at the window. There was an acacia tree beyond the ash, its trunk split and twisted. But he had never heard of acacia furniture. Next door there was a pear tree.

"It could be fruit wood of some kind," he suggested cautiously. "You know, apple wood or pear. They have a very fine grained wood like this."

"Pretty big fruit trees. Look at the apple tree in your garden. You couldn't make a chair leg out of that, let alone a cupboard."

Anna had been moving about behind them. Suddenly

they heard a click and both jumped round – Hugh momentarily surprised that he could be so easily startled, though
Penn, he noticed, moved just as warily. Anna was standing
by the cupboard. She was expressionless, but the cupboard
doors were closed.

At that moment came another sound and Jean walked in.
"What a *mess*," she said briskly. And indeed, books, clothes,
papers, were strewn everywhere. Hugh thought he must
have slept very untidily as well, because the blankets were
half off his unmade bed, and he noticed footmarks on the
sheets where his slippers had been, which he covered hastily
and guiltily.

"That doesn't make it look any better, Hugh," said Jean in
her primmest voice.

Penn had Anna by the shoulder and was shaking her.

"What did you do, Anna? Why did you shut the cupboard?"

"I put something in. I wanted to see."

"What, Anna, what did you put in?"

"Whatever's *happening?*" begged Jean.

"It was Hugh's sweater; your red woollen one."

"My wallet was leather; pigskin," shouted Hugh, at last
remembering it.

"*Pig* skin," said Anna, with triumph in her voice.

"I suppose you think," said Penn sarcastically, "I suppose
you think —"

"Wool comes from sheep," Jean cried excitedly.

"Well, fancy, as if we didn't know," said Hugh.

"Well, Anna, are you expecting a sheep now?" But
though Penn's voice was light, amused, he and all of them
turned simultaneously to stare at the cupboard doors.

"I can't hear anything," said Jean after a moment, tentatively.

"Did you expect to? I bet nothing happens at all."

But they watched the cupboard, all of them. They waited painfully, anxiously – in hope – fear – anxiety that something would or would not come out of it. They waited for such sounds as they had heard yesterday, but there was only the commonplace chirping of the sparrows in the ash tree and the low plaint of a car coming up the road. (Hugh could tell it was up, not down, because cars going down made lighter sounds that disappeared more quickly.) The front gate clashed behind the milkman. They heard the whine and rattle of the red milk truck.

Penn looked at Anna triumphantly; stared round, boldly, at the rest of them. Then he marched to the cupboard and pulled open the door. No red sweater lay on the shelf now, where Anna must have put it, only a heap of fluff such as a sheep leaves behind in a hedge; except that there was more of it and yellow; the sheep must have been recently dipped.

"You see," said Anna. "You see, Penn?"

"And you put a woollen sweater in? Are you mad, Anna? We might have got a sheep. Coping with that pig was just about enough."

"A moment ago you were saying nothing would happen. You can't have it all ways, Penn," said Hugh.

"Poor Anna," Jean said.

But Anna had begun to laugh. A moment later so had Hugh and Jean, and then, after staring round all of them in turn, slightly red-faced, rather indignant, Penn followed too, if not with much amusement. Hugh was watching Anna more; slightly pink, dishevelled, laughing, she looked quite different suddenly. She noticed his eyes and turned away, jerking her head down sideways, so that hair fell across her eyes, and when Hugh saw her face again all the colour had ebbed, leaving it as usual pale and quenched by the short, unsuitable, black dress.

They retired to the garden shortly afterwards. The sky was entirely blue, and the sun beginning to be hot. They lay full in the sun, near the old climbing frame which had half its rungs missing and leaned at an angle of forty-five degrees. Jean's cat got up from it when they appeared and took to the more adequate shade that was made by Hugh.

Penn, though still noticeably annoyed with Anna, had regained his composure and was at his bossiest, suggesting what he called a controlled experiment. They should each, he said, bring a selection of objects to put in the cupboard; they would see then what came out of it. They would have to be careful, naturally. There were things made from animals much more dangerous than pigs.

"No elephant's feet," said Jean, inclined to giggle still.

Hugh irritated by Penn took up the game at once.

"Or leopard skin."

"Or shark's teeth necklaces," said Jean.

"Sharks wouldn't be dangerous unless they brought the sea as well," said Hugh.

"Do you remember the one in the Natural History Museum? That's huge. One that size would split up the cupboard walls."

"It would split my room."

"Suppose it wouldn't get into the cupboard in the first place?" said Jean.

"How would we ever manage to explain a shark?"

Anna said nothing. Penn stiffly, red with annoyance, said they weren't here to talk about sharks, and what time would they meet that afternoon to try the cupboard out?

"No," said Hugh violently. "Not this afternoon."

"But why ever not."

"It's my room, my cupboard, isn't it? No, no, no."

Penn was silent for a moment. Both Jean and Anna appeared asleep, while Hugh stroked the cat frenetically. After a moment it twisted from his hands and went. Penn changed his tactics, began most uncharacteristically slowly, patiently.

"But look, Hugh, you can't leave everything lying round your room much longer. Suppose your mother comes up."

"She never does."

"Just occasionally she does," added Jean, from where she lay apparently asleep.

"She's just as likely to be suspicious if we're up there all afternoon on a day like this."

"She's never suspicious. She never bothers to be."

"She does bother," Hugh almost shouted, then added in a lower voice, "I don't want to do it this afternoon, I tell you. I just don't want to. It is my room, isn't it?"

"So you've already said," agreed Penn. But Hugh's agitation had neatly calmed his. "All right, all right," he was saying amiably. "Not this afternoon. Tomorrow then. Who cares?"

It took Hugh a moment to realise he had won his point, and he was left bewildered, mentally unsteady. It was like pushing all your weight against a door which then opened easily, leaving you staggering.

CHAPTER 6

HUGH lay on his back, gazing up into the sky, feeling the prickle of grasses under him. They had come to the park for the afternoon, all four of them. The girls did not usually accompany the boys but now whatever they did or did not do seemed related in some way to the cupboard – rather as a shadow belongs inextricably to the solid object from which it falls. Everything seemed necessarily to involve all of them, even when it did not actually involve the cupboard.

Anna, however, had complained of a headache after a while, somewhat whinily; a migraine she had called it.

"You're always having headaches," Penn said brutally, but when Anna had set off for home in search of aspirin he had watched her across the grass till she was out of sight, a thin, small, curiously solitary figure.

There were willow trees, four of them by an empty stream, one bent almost parallel to the ground. Penn sat astride this as if it was a horse, while Jean, a little pink in the face at having Penn all to herself, leaned against the same tree.

"Migraine is awful," Hugh heard her say, from where he lay separate. "One of the mistresses at school has migraines. She has a terrible headache and she can't see anything; just a little pin point is all she sees."

A pin point; a little pin point, Hugh thought. He was looking up into the sky. He felt – for the vast sky was nothing to his eyes, invisible layers of air and atmosphere – as if his vision had narrowed to some little point, which he could not decipher immediately, and after a while with staring up

his eyes seemed to be making rings of air, as water looks
when a stone falls and ripples spread about; except that these
rings moved inward, centripetally. He moved his eyes away,
sideways, into grass. The stems were magnified, juicy, huge.
When he looked up again the speck, the pin point, was
nearer, had resolved itself into a hawk, hovering. Even from
such a height it could, he knew, see things move among these
same grass stems. It continued hovering with blurry wings –
the moment, held, appeared an hour. Then suddenly it
stooped, fell, but jerked itself up before reaching earth,
veered off, with slow and easy strokes.

"A kestrel," Hugh heard Jean telling Penn. But she only
knew because he, Hugh, had pointed kestrels out to her at
other times. They had left the willow tree and were desul-
torily playing cricket, Penn solo in effect, diving, catching,
exercising himself. From where Hugh lay, if grass looked
like trees Penn looked like a giant.

Hugh, his face burning, eased himself back till he lay
partly screened by bracken. The sky looked blue again and
was cut by the little teeth of the bracken fronds. There was a
sharp, green smell, and tickings from insects he could not
see. The cricket bat flashed into corners of his vision, but
though he searched the sky he could not see the kestrel any
more and so he shut his eyes, let his thinking narrow to a
single point; a point he had pursued, yet avoided, all day
long.

He thought of dreams; that flowed in your mind when it
was freed by sleep, but always remained inside your mind,
did not involve physical, breakable bones and flesh and
skin.

But this world he had been into twice had made him cold;
it had made him wet, so it could not be a dream world. It had
to be altogether another world, another time, like Thomas

the Rhymer's fairyland, where a man lived for years while no time passed in his own world. Or else – and at thought of this Hugh contracted with fear – or else he emerged from it after what seemed but a few days, and found that hundreds of years had gone by; so that he was a stranger, out of time.

But if it had not been a dream, the reality he had experienced had been of a different kind. It was as if everything he knew had been taken apart and then put together in a different way, in a pattern just as agreeable yet apparently wayward, because it was not the pattern in which he normally lived. He might follow it in time but it would take him time to do that; as eyes take time to adjust from light to dark.

It was a world, Hugh thought, in which animals, trees, landmarks were not just animals or trees or landmarks, but friends or enemies, or both at once. He remembered suddenly, vividly, the alder trees, that had surrounded him like friends, but then tried to hinder his going, like enemies. And the birch trees – once when Hugh looked back they had seemed peaceful, harmonious, like slender peaceful women; but the next moment they had appeared as warriors, with twigs and branches for arrows and for spears.

It all came back to Hugh now, what had happened to him last night. What dream he'd had. It was not a dream, he knew, but he did not know what else to call it. And that evening, Monday, when he found himself back in this other place, it was as if he had never been away.

Light came slowly. He was still walking through the same bleak landscape, towards the same castle, which looked farther away than ever, because now Hugh could see, between it and him, the deep folds in the country that he would have to traverse. There was one fold immediately below him. A group of willow trees stood at the centre of it, beside a little stream.

The snow was patchier than it had seemed at night and the land beneath it, tired and brown and dim, was made drearier if anything by the strengthening daylight. The light was at the same time strong yet bleak; it bleached out the castle which no longer looked as if it was made of glass. It looked more like a castle made of bone.

Hugh went downwards now, into the hollow with the willow trees. The slope cut off the castle bit by bit, until he could see only the topmost battlements, and then not even them, for the hollow, engulfing him, wiped out the land-scape. There was only sky and the remains of bracken, sodden and brown and patched with coarse, greyish-looking snow. There was also the group of willow trees.

Hugh put out a hand and touched a willow tree. The bark was pitted, coarse and lined. He stroked it, feeling still more roughness than his eyes saw, and when his hand slowed, it took a moment for him to realise that he had not meant to slow it; that his brain had not ordered nerve, nerve had not ordered muscle, even subconsciously. The hand had seemed to slow, stop, entirely of its own accord. It was as if it had frozen. And when he touched the tree with his other hand he found that that at once was frozen too, that he could not move either hand, that indeed he could not move at all.

His brain searched out each nerve to command each muscle. But he could not sort out one from another, work out which muscle controlled which limb. He was frozen totally.

It was then that he realised there was another traveller, a man on horseback. But he was moving, he came on – Hugh heard him for considerably longer than he saw him – the jingle of harness, the clod and thump of feet on bracken. Not only could he not turn his head to see, he found that now he could not even move his eyes. They were fixed in one focus, confined to a single plane, as if he looked out from the narrowest of windows. The man passed across it briefly, and so near that Hugh saw pieces only of man and horse, not the whole at once. He did not see the man's face, and the man entirely ignored him. The sound of his going went on for a long time afterwards.

The next thing Hugh knew was his own bed. He lay in it frozen still, uncertain still how to make any movement. He felt huge, edgeless, like a landscape in which the lines of his body formed the folds and dips and ridges. Cautiously he began testing nerves; fitting muscle to limb; moving head, hands, body, and in turn each arm and leg; rolled over in bed at last, wallowing hugely, and fell asleep with a heavy sigh.

CHAPTER 7

"It's *not* plastic, it's leather," said Jean. "*Real* leather. You said we mustn't put in leather things."

"It isn't leather. It's imitation. Smell it. Leather doesn't smell like that," said Penn.

"But it looks like leather."

"It's plastic and it looks like plastic."

"What is plastic, anyway?" asked Hugh to calm the two of them. But no one really knew, when they considered it. Hugh dug up the word synthetic but that led them nowhere beyond itself. "We know it's not an animal, only chemicals of some sort," said Penn, "so at least it's safe to put it in and see."

"Look I tell you Penn, you are not to have my one and only purse, even if it is plastic. And I think it's leather any-way."

"So where's your spirit of inquiry, Jean?" asked Penn.

"There's some plastic ducks in the bathroom, we could use them instead," suggested Hugh.

"Hughie's bath toys, I suppose?"

"They're from when we were *little*," Jean said. And it was true their mother rarely, if ever, threw anything away, let alone sorted things. Downstairs in the hall, stratified by age like rock, hung layers and layers of clothes that Jean and Hugh had worn, going back to the days before they went to school; the bulk tending to reject any current garment hung too carelessly on top of them, so that Hugh invariably went to school in a blazer that had sat on the floor all night. Jean had given up long ago and kept her coats always in her room.

Hugh returned from the bathroom with a pair of dented and faded and dusty ducks to find that Penn, meanwhile, had seized Jean's purse after all and flung it in the cupboard. He pushed aside the feeling that he ought to be indignant on Jean's behalf – he did not actually feel indignant at all – in his interest at what might emerge. But when they pulled open the cupboard doors they found only an oily and malodourous liquid, slightly warm and definitely unpleasant, reflecting acid colours not to be found in the room. Jean, neat-stepped, tight-lipped, straight-backed, went down to the bathroom in her turn to fetch a cloth to wipe this up; but first plucked the plastic ducks from Hugh and hurled them at Penn, who fielded with utmost nonchalance, at the same time saying rather indignantly to Hugh, "We need a scientist round here. Why aren't you a scientist, Hugh?" – the kind of unhelpful remark Hugh's father more usually made to him.

Penn and Anna had brought from home a torn supermarket carrier stuffed with odds and ends; a comb with a few teeth left, a ripped and moulting Davy Crockett hat ("How about ducks now?" Jean muttered on its appearance, but Penn did not bother noticing, let alone taking offence), a fleet of matchbox cars lacking most of their paint, newspapers, handkerchiefs, a box of matches, a painted wooden horse minus two legs, a china dog, a glass mug, a tin plate, a chipped china bowl; even a toothpaste tube with a little toothpaste left; also nails, screws, bits of string and thread and wire. It looked as if Penn had chosen carefully at first, then chucked in everything that he could find.

Jean contributed a small tortoise-shell box, and she and Hugh together had brought a large mahogany box with a small brass inlay at the centre of the lid. It was Jean's idea. Hugh, feeling that he had already provided more than his fair share, had sorted out all the things he particularly cared about, painting things mostly, paints, brushes, canvasses and drawing-pads, kept unlike his clothes in impeccable order, and hidden them all in his bottom drawer, turning the clothes out on to the top of the chest.

"Mum never uses the button box," Jean said. "In this house it's me that sews buttons on."

The box had sat in the bottom drawer of a huge oak tallboy as long as Hugh could remember. When little he had sometimes played with it for hours, devising button pictures and button patterns. It gave him a sense of curious displacement touching these buttons again now – a sense of loss almost – of time perhaps, but more, of himself.

They dated generations back; there were modern plastic buttons, brass buttons, plain or with anchors on, almost all tarnished; velvet-covered buttons, the velvet mostly split and faded; smooth round pearl buttons, flat, subtler mother-of-pearl buttons; some large white buttons minutely carved. "These are bone, I think," said Hugh. "We'd better be careful." "What sort of bone?" asked Jean. "How should I know," Hugh said. "How about whalebone?" suggested Penn. "I say we don't find out," said Hugh. He and Penn looked at each other and laughed and threw punches, aimed at, but not meeting, flesh.

Hugh picked a bone button from the box. Its carvings must have needed a point of needle size; they made an intricate, geometric pattern that he thought entirely abstract at first glance. But then, as he was examining it, it was as if his eyes changed focus suddenly. The pattern shifted, jumped out at him – however hard he tried he could not blink it away again. For there was a castle; flattened, one-dimensional, but a castle nonetheless with lines indicating battlements and the dimensions of hewn stone blocks.

All the bone buttons were similar. On each a castle now came to eye. Though Hugh hunted feverishly he could not find one without. Meanwhile, the familiar clack, clink, slither of the buttons revived other familiarities. The bone buttons had always been in the box, he remembered. Even the castles were not as strange to him as he had thought initially. Recognition of memory came, then memory of knowing them. Yet he did not lose his sense of shock. Bone buttons. Castles of bone, he thought. "Just suppose they were made of human bone," said Penn.

But it was hard to tell of what many things were made. The Davy Crockett hat, for instance, could have been rabbit or cat or even nylon. "It's certainly never seen a racoon," said Hugh. They were very careful at first, trying only the most obvious materials. A box of matches became a small fir tree with its roots still full of earth. ("What a pity it isn't Christmas," Jean said, but it was an uneven tree, much bushier on one side than the other. Hugh would never have chosen it from a shop.) A brass button emerged from the cupboard as two small pieces of rock, one greyish, one yellower, that Hugh explained held zinc and copper ore before metal had been smelted out of stone.

"Man, ain't this educational," said Penn. "But not just educational," Anna said quietly. And it was not indeed. You did not, in merely acquiring knowledge, wait with such a shiver between question and answer. You did not impose ritual, such as they imposed on themselves at first. Someone would advance alone, place an object on a shelf and close the door, the gentleness or firmness of that depending on who it was; Penn for instance decisive, Jean brisk, yet a little hesitant. Anna was quite as decisive as Penn, Hugh thought, but in a very different way; slower, more deliberate, prolonging each moment and giving it weight. He himself tried to shut the doors so quietly that there was no click at all. Silence in this seemed to him aesthetically necessary, even satisfying.

Then they would wait, silent and intent. Light in these moments took on almost the quality of sound for Hugh, while sound had a grainy texture to his ears, as if he could touch and see, as well as hear it. Sometimes, waiting, he felt no tension. Sometimes, for no apparent reason, with no apparent difference, the tension was unbearable. He noticed Anna watching him once. He had been scratching his groin, only half consciously, and hastily he moved his hand. The movement broke the thread, for him, for everyone. Someone opened the cupboard door. This time a white cotton handkerchief had turned into a plant with a fluffy, untidy head.

"Everything has stages of development," Penn said. "But we don't know which stage the cupboard is going to choose. It takes things back to any stage, you can never predict what."

"Hugh's wallet turned back into a pig itself. His sweater didn't become a sheep," said Jean.

"If you put a person in," said Anna, smiling at Hugh, "a person of thirty, say, they would come out a baby or a child, or even a younger grownup. And you wouldn't know which in advance."

"That's exactly it." Hugh felt Penn watching him smile back at Anna.

"That's exactly what I meant. How about trying a person then," Penn said. "You would do fine, Hugh." He nudged Hugh, a nudge perhaps sharper than necessary. Hugh might have protested or retaliated had not the cupboard at that moment illustrated the point exactly, by returning for the chewed and twisted toothpaste tube, instead of a heap of materials, a new tube, shiny, plump and full. It might have come straight from the manufacturers.

All of them suddenly became lit and warm and wild. They rolled about with laughter, as if someone had made a particularly funny joke. But the excitement was dangerous, frosty-edged, a little hysterical. The tortoise-shell box became actually a tortoise with blinking eyes and a prehistoric scaly skin – the first live creature to emerge from the cupboard since the white sow itself – which so fired Penn that he grabbed Hugh's one silk scarf from an open drawer, and let the cupboard turn it into a silkworm, little as a pin. None of them could find this at first, it was so small, and while they hunted on hands and knees, Jean, enraged about the scarf and still angry about her purse, seized, from the back pocket of his jeans, Penn's diary, in which he put the dates of his cricket and football games. It emerged from the cupboard an unattractive mixture of wood-pulp and oil. "So *that* wasn't leather-covered either, Penn," she said. Hugh thought Penn might actually hit Jean then. He towered; his fist was raised, his face on fire.

From then on they seemed to be arguing all the time. Penn accused Jean of being officious; Jean accused Penn of bossiness. Hugh was distracted, felt apart and unhelpful, succeeded only in being clumsy. Anna said almost nothing but carried on exactly in her own way. She irrationally but quite profoundly irritated Hugh, who dismissed the feeling as one of the many he had these days that seemed much too large and unwieldy for whatever had aroused it.

Ritual first blurred, then entirely disappeared. They started to shove everything into the cupboard at once. Newspapers and buttons, string and nails emerged in pointless, unpromising heaps, from which it would have been impossible to disentangle the origins of anything. As Hugh raked out the whole lot rather angrily on to the bedroom floor, his sister Jean turned uncharacteristically perhaps the wildest of them all, rushed away downstairs, returning a little later with raisins, dried beans, a box of salt, and a jar of meat extract with a bull's head on its label. "Well you can ditch that for a start," said Penn.

Hugh took the raisins from her hands. They were actually muscatels, in a three-cornered box, very wrinkled and dried up. He put them into the cupboard and closed the door on them just as his mother walked in, panting a little from the climb up four flights of stairs.

She stood in the doorway shouting. She wore a brown cotton skirt with a split in one seam and the hem halfway down the same side. Her hair must have been newly washed the way it flew out from her head, with a blur of little lights round the edge of it. She never had the smooth, the polished look, that Hugh thought other people's mothers had.

And there they were: Hugh standing by the cupboard, with his hand on the catch; Jean, flushed and unusually rakish and untidy-looking, holding a box of best sea salt; Penn leaning nonchalantly against the window, his body distorting a beam of light; Anna sitting on Hugh's unmade bed, holding the little fir-tree from which she plucked needles and crushed them between her fingers. Hugh's nose caught wafts of their small strong pungencies. His mother looked oddly at Anna, looked at her twice, but did not speak, as if she could not quite analyse why what she saw was strange. Then she swept across the room and pulled open the cupboard door.

"Grapes. *Grapes.*"

"I bought them," Hugh said hastily.

"Come buy," said Penn, "all fresh, all sweet."

"Who'll buy . . ." Jean's voice started on a high note,

split, fell into helpless giggles. They were particularly lush, fat, purple grapes, lying on a heap of wood shavings. Hugh's mother ate three before letting fly at Hugh again.

How could he have had the cupboard since Sunday (Saturday, muttered Hugh) and not put anything away in it? How could he have such a mess in his room? What were grapes of all things doing in his cupboard? (She ate another three.) As she went on Hugh's anger mounted, was beginning to match hers, until he saw Penn giggling ostentatiously behind her back. Then he turned his anger, bent it against Penn, let most evaporate in a single glare.

But when, her rage faltering, she had gone, they all fell on and devoured the bunch of grapes. And all, including Hugh, lay round the floor giggling hysterically.

"You must admit it's a problem," Penn said finally.

"What problem?" asked Hugh, suspiciously.

"To have a cupboard you can't use as a cupboard. If you put all your clothes away as your mother said, you'd be nude; you wouldn't be decent to go in the street. So what are you going to do? She's bound to come back again." They all collapsed once more at the thought of Hugh's nakedness.

"Oh I'll hide them; stuff them away somewhere and keep the cupboard shut; then she won't know it's empty."

"You can't get away with it for ever," said Jean.

"Well, we'd better make some effort to tidy now." Penn climbed to his feet, brushing himself down. "No more cupboard, not for now. All hands to clearing up the place. Get up, Anna, you lazy little beast."

Anna had been lying under the window on her back, with her eyes closed. She did not stir at first when Penn poked her with his foot. Then slowly and deliberately she opened her eyes wide, and a moment later raised herself on an elbow.

She must have been lying on that hand. Its skin had taken on the ridges of the worn cord carpet.

"Get up, lazybones," said Penn. "Get up and help."

Anna giggled. "It's not my room. I'm not going to."

"You are, you know."

"I'm not, you know."

"You jolly well something *are*." Penn grabbed her under the armpits and began to heave. She left him all her weight and annoyed, he grew rougher, dragging her. "You're *hurting*," Anna said.

"Get up then."

"No." Anna laughed again.

"*Get* up!" Penn shook her furiously. She stopped laughing abruptly, set her feet down, wriggled round, lashed out, fought with him, Penn's greater strength quite matched by her fury.

"She was hurting, really scratching," Jean said to Hugh afterwards. "And kicking. Did you see? I've never kicked you like that, or scratched."

"Well, he was brutish enough too. But you wouldn't call her timid exactly. I always used to think her timid. She scarcely opened her mouth at all."

"But she is still timid, in a funny sort of way," said Jean.

The fight had stopped as suddenly as it began. Anna froze, looking at Penn's watch. "Oh Lord, oh dear, it's after one already. I promised Mummy I'd be home to help with lunch." She seemed all anxiety and awkwardness, and left without picking up a thing.

Penn bellowed down the stairway after her. "When we try putting a human in the cupboard, it'll be you, Anna. You'll be the guinea-pig, if you don't damn well watch out."

CHAPTER 8

HUGH, gazing out of the window after lunch, saw Penn and Anna turn out of their gate and up the road. He spent a great deal of time gazing out of his window. It amused and occupied him at least when he had nothing else to do or when a painting was going badly, and at most it left him with an extraordinary, strange, creative ache; a beautiful yet unbearable sense of growing out of himself, exploding skin and bone. He tried to catch this feeling sometimes, record it, pin it down. But always at once it faded, or collapsed like a blown-up paper bag.

It gave him a pleasing sense of power too, gazing out of his window. He felt god-like – seeing people who did not see him scratch themselves, or mutter or gesture dramatically, unaware of being watched, people with whom he had no need to involve himself, as merely passing in the street he would have had to be involved. Like a god he felt above time even, anticipating events. He knew for instance now that the car nipping so busily along the road was about to be brought up short behind a trail of cars barred by an oil-delivery tank; and again seeing a poodle shut up in a parked car, a large Alsatian approaching on a lead foretold an enjoyable eruption of which no one else was yet aware.

Anna and Penn were just ahead of the dog, walking slowly, their heads together. Whatever did they always have to say to each other, Hugh wondered, with annoyance. In company Anna was so silent usually and Penn critical of her or teasing.

The poodle sprang against its window barking furiously. The Alsatian leaped explosively, thunderously, almost dragged its startled owner down. Penn and Anna jumped apart, Anna scuttling in at the gate, Penn almost scuttling too, but then pausing and shaking himself and walking in with dignity, while Hugh laughed himself silly in strangely malicious triumph and amusement.

"I saw it coming a mile off," he explained.

"I saw it too," said Penn aggressively.

"Rubbish," said Anna, "neither of us did."

"Well are you ready, Hugh, anyway?" Penn asked.

They were going to the Royal Tournament, a military display; not a function Hugh would have chosen for himself or indeed any of them, except Penn just possibly.

"It's hardly for pacifists," Hugh commented.

"Well I'm not a pacifist. Why? Are you?"

"I'm thinking of it. I was last term."

"I bet you're not. Rubbish. It's just affectation."

Penn's father had been given four tickets by some business acquaintance. "It's free entertainment, isn't it?" Penn said. "It won't entertain me in the slightest," protested Hugh, and indeed when he walked into the exhibition hall that afternoon and saw tanks and guns lined up, the array of dowdy yet lethal armaments, he almost retreated and went home at once.

He resisted everything at first; the marching, the patterns made by the marchers on the arena floor; the sound patterns made by the armorial bands. He felt that disliking the belligerence for which these stood, he ought not to allow shivers to run up and down his back. Yet he could not have come to an event more suited to his, to all their present states of mind, because of the noise and glare and ritual; and though he did not want to be carried away and lost, he soon fell into a state of dream which came dangerously near to it.

Looking down on the arena, an oval of orange sand, Hugh

felt above time again, anticipating events; except that here, the formations moving, advancing against each other, he would have anticipated collision rather than their actual neat enfolding, row on row, each rank sliding whole through others and emerging whole. The lights changed ceaselessly. The troops were all green one moment, then white, then pink, then scarlet, then all colours together at once. The lights and music jointly hypnotised him. By the time the gun race started – two teams of sailors from different naval ports dragging guns and gun-carriages over an obstacle course – he was yelling like everyone else and totally overcome. And when it ended, with a crash of cannons and a cloud of bitter smoke which touched their faces and hung pale against the darkness overhead, as against a tangible, solid surface, the pleasure he felt was out of proportion to the event. He seemed to explode with light and relief and joy.

"Well, I think we can say that went off with a bang, ladies and gentlemen," said the voice of the avuncular colonel in the commentator's box. Penn and Hugh looked at each other derisively, shrieked with irreverent laughter. They leaned across Jean and Anna who were sitting between them and shook hands solemnly.

"What an absolutely *sooper* bang," they said all but simultaneously, with exaggerated army accents. Just as Hugh came out of cinemas feeling bold or reflective or poetical, according to the film, so now he took his mood from the tournament. He felt splendid suddenly, glittering, a match for Penn any day, using words for weapons, flinging them along the row, across both Jean and Anna. "Don't mind us," said Jean indignantly. And twice, somebody behind Hugh leaned over and tapped his shoulder and told him, authoritatively, to keep still, be quiet.

"And now," proclaimed the relentless jolly colonel, "we

offer you a dangerous and stunning event. Every week, ladies and gentlemen, these brave teams suffer a broken bone or two, practising on your behalf, to entertain you now. We present to you, proudly, on motor-cycles, the Army Daredevils!"

The stadium suddenly went black. The sour smell of horse urine drifted up from the arena floor. People waited, rustled, coughed a little. A roaring grew from somewhere – lights went up suddenly – it was as if that made sound as well as light, for the noise grew furious, the great doors flew away; with a roar and a rush in dashed a chain of motor-cycles – two, three chains, one behind the other; black motor-cycles, black-clad riders. They roared to the far end of the arena and back again, split, wheeled round and rode diagonally across each other, missing by hairs'-breadths, then returned with mighty, restrengthening roars. Even sceptical Hugh held his breath anxiously.

"Want some more, gentlemen?" inquired the colonel.

"*No*," yelled Hugh and Penn together, and looked at each other grinning. "They'll crash, they'll crash," Jean was saying frantically. "Oh I wish they'd stop." But Anna seemed to like it as much as Hugh and Penn. She gripped the seat, her face open, full of life.

"You haven't seen anything *yet*," bellowed the commentator. "Now for a mid-air crossover," – and then in a moment, when it was over – "Want it again?" he asked.

"Oh I hate it, they'll crash," wailed Jean, as the motor-cycles dashed once more on their opposite diagonals, rode up ramps and jumped, missing others by inches in mid-air.

"*Miss*," whispered Penn. "Come on, *miss*," whispered Hugh, and heard an echo, it must have been Anna, sighing "Miss . . . miss . . . miss."

Jean watched no more, just turned miserably away. When

52

the cyclists, having crashed through walls and leapt through hoops of fire, departed at last, leaving an obtrusive silence and petrol fumes, her relief broke out in furious irritation.

"I'm sick of you leaning all over me, Hugh. If you and Penn have to be so stupid, why don't you just sit together. I'll move up."

She shuffled along into Hugh's place while he climbed over her. But there was still a space on her other side. Anna simply had not moved at all. Hugh looked at her, puzzled, and waited for her.

"Budge up, Anna, there's a love," he said to her at last.

"Budge *up*, Ann," hissed Penn more urgently. A new event was expected in the lit arena. From behind came murmurings, protests, as people shifted and craned their heads.

"Sit down, will you," ordered a louder voice, behind.

Hugh, desperate, climbed over Anna as much as it was possible, Penn beyond having squeezed up as far as he could. They earned more disapproving glares from Penn's other neighbour, but Anna still had not moved at all. Since the motor-cycles went a light might have gone out in her. She gazed straight ahead, expressionless. Hugh sat down firmly anyway, partly on Anna, partly on Penn, which was effectively uncomfortable, for Anna shifted, only fractionally, but enough for him to fit, just, into the space between her and Penn. Her eyes never strayed from the arena once. She sat very straight and held hands demurely with herself, her left thumb tucked inside her right fist, the fingers folded on top of it. Hugh noticed a tell-tale chewing movement in her cheek.

Then at last he looked back to the arena. And saw what, despite newly added props, had been there all the time. And yet he had not consciously taken it in. It was as if till now he had not been allowed to take it in; it was as if, just as with the button box, his eyes had refocused, slightly shifted vision. He saw a castle, another castle.

He leaned over the still unyielding Anna and snatching the programme they had bought from Jean, leafed through pages of advertisements to find the table of events. "Event Number Twelve. The Attack," it said. "The seige and storming of an English Castle. A re-enactment of mediaeval warfare, staged and presented by Colonel Bassett-Brown M.C."

Hugh returned the programme to the indignant Jean and looked back into the arena; at what his eyes, his mind and something less obvious had contrived to keep from his consciousness. There was a crudely painted castle on the end arena wall, around and above the entrance doors. It was two-dimensional, apart from turrets on either side, battlements that jutted a little way into the arena and a drawbridge across a simulated moat. Three-dimensional, it would, however, have been a square castle.

The teams of men working in the arena fell into line now, and in line ran off. The light changed, dramatised itself. To the sound of trumpets an army entered from the opposite end of the arena, headed by a man on a black horse bearing a standard. His armour was silver, but his flag, shield and tunic were a dark holly green with scarlet devices on them. Archers appeared on the castle battlements. The drawbridge was lifted. The invaders brought scaling ladders and a batter-ing ram. The attack on the castle began.

Hugh never doubted that the attack would succeed and could not remember subsequently a single detail; only the curious relief he felt when the castle had been stormed and taken. ("It isn't a patch on Ivanhoe," Penn whispered in his ear. "Now that *was* a proper castle.") He did not understand why its capture should seem so crucial, nor why he should feel such relief, since he already knew the outcome. Yet he did feel relief. It carried him through the rest of the pro-gramme in a dream, scarcely noticing any of it, his ears still filled with the triumph of trumpets, his eyes with the glitter and fierceness of steel points and blades. The castle was flat again, amateurishly painted, yet still to his mind and memory it was stone, four-square and strong against invasion and attack, the picture in his mind more powerful than the one before his eyes.

He dreamed that night; indeed he not only expected, he forced this dream, or had the illusion that he did. He felt all-powerful. He took the holly trees along the fence in their garden, rearranged them in his mind, and sure enough found himself beside a line of holly trees on a hilltop, looking down on the castle now, or so it seemed.

He was close enough to see it in more detail than before. Trees stood near it, leafless still, and the wind blew mightily and threw the trees about. It looked almost as if the castle standing among them turned, spun, as if it revolved on a spool or plinth. There were bushes as well as trees crouched close to the ground like animals – like lions, Hugh thought. Some were bolt upright, some lay flat, yet all were wakeful, watchful. The roaring of the wind sounded like the lions roaring. The whole landscape seemed to have come to life about Hugh today.

And then he saw a man below him galloping towards the castle. It was the man he had seen before, but there was a glitter about him now. Bit, bridle, sword and spear gave off little points of light. Hugh thought he heard sounds from them, clinks, glitters and jinglings, just as he had thought he heard the roaring lions.

Horse and man galloped in slow motion at first, uphill, but they quickened rapidly, the slope levelling out. As they swept faster and faster across the ground, Hugh began running too, stumbling over the prickly grass, while the castle turned in front of him. He thought he saw men on the battlements now, archers with bent bows. He could have sworn there were roaring lions all round. Watching the castle instead of his step, as he gasped for breath, he lost footing, stumbled and fell, banging his head severely. He lay with the sky, the earth, the whole world spinning and turning about, then within, his head, then found himself lying giddily, in darkness, in warmth, in his own bed.

He stilled the spinning deliberately by turning between the sheets. Something prickled him through his pyjamas. He put his hand down and the same something was prickling his hand, several places at once across one small area of skin. He pulled out a holly leaf and threw it on to the floor beside his bed.

CHAPTER 9

NEXT morning Hugh provided the forgotten tortoise with a cardboard box and some lettuce leaves. Then he set up an experiment. He had woken with a passionate desire for knowledge; not simply to watch the cupboard working as they had done yesterday, but to understand the mechanics, how and why it worked. Just as he always wanted to paint alone, so now he wanted to do this alone. He peered over the bannister on their landing to make sure that Jean was not on her way upstairs, and then closed the door very quietly and carefully.

The box of buttons was beneath his bed. Hugh pulled it out, opened and searched through it carefully until he found three brass buttons, all identical except that one was less tarnished than the other two. This one Hugh chose to put in the cupboard first, shutting the door on it. He timed the interval by the second hand on his watch and after thirty seconds exactly opened the cupboard again.

The second button he left for a minute on the same shelf; the third for one minute and twenty seconds. The first button emerged like the button the day before, two lumps of rock veined just decipherably with metal. The second was still a button, but infinitely shinier, as if new from the maker's mould. The third button, left in longest, came out smelted, liquid, hot. Hugh burnt his fingers and swore out loud as the metal cooled and hardened before his eyes.

Rummaging in the button box he managed to find a fourth brass button, with an anchor on it, just as the others had. He left this in for the same length of time as he had the

57

third, but it emerged only as two lumps of stone, like the button he had left for half a minute only.

He concluded then that you could not control this past at all; that is, you could not determine the stage of its past to which you wanted some object to revert, by the length of time you left it in the cupboard. The cupboard worked to its own timings, had its own logic. It would have comforted Hugh a little to have disproved that, if only minimally. If time as he knew it, running in a straight line, from the past through the present to the future, had related to the cupboard, even in reverse, it would have been something to cling to, to make him feel safe. It must be orthodox time, he thought, which made life seem relatively stable and ordinary. If time melted, had no force, then space, the whole physical world could easily melt as well. Hugh longed for one aspect of the cupboard to be controllable.

He stood staring at it, as if the cupboard itself, its wood, its form, might divulge some of its reason and purposes. He held a door open with one hand and rested his other hand on a shelf. He was stretched across the cupboard, his arms wide, but the cupboard seemed to hold him, rather than he it. The sun flowed past him, round him, bringing out the close grain of the wood (so close that to the naked eye it scarcely made patterns on the wood, as coarser graining does). Light brought out the differential tarnishing of the thin brass hanging-rail. In one place he could see all colours there, oily rainbow colours like the colours of the melted plastic.

Hugh dropped his hands suddenly and stepped right back. He clenched his hands and stood perfectly still, his head singing curiously. He took one step forward – hesitated – pulled his foot back.

He wanted – he could not look at what he wanted, because he knew that he must not, should not do it. But he wanted to; only, he was afraid. He put his foot forward again; he could not help it, it might have been dragged; and snatched it back. And again he could not help it, for his fear took over. He felt the two contrary pulls that he had felt before, himself ruling neither, yet ruled by both. They cancelled one another now and left him motionless.

He wanted to get inside the cupboard. There was a little, clear, moving picture inside his head of stepping in, crushing himself up, pulling the doors shut on himself. The doors snapped across his mind, cutting off pictures, making his eyes blind. It was dark inside the cupboard. The brass rail sang above him. He could see nothing now, only feel it.

Darkness. Hugh shook his head. For there was no darkness, only full daylight, hot sun. He stood staring at the cupboard, and the wanting to enter it was still so strong it pulled him forward. He took one step forward and another, telling himself it was only to retrieve the pool of hardened metal that still lay on the floor in front of the cupboard. He bent, reached out a hand, stepped forward again. One foot was actually in the cupboard now. In a moment the rest of him would have followed. But —

"Hugh, *Hugh*," came a voice behind him and the crash of an opening door. "Penn and Anna are here. Mum says we ought to go. She'll take us down to the station."

"I don't believe she's ready, for a start." Hugh's voice belonged to someone else. His eyes blinked in the sunlight.

"Well she is, for once. You'd better hurry up," said Jean. "Well I'm not."

"Well hurry up. What have you been doing, Hugh?"

"It's far too late to go anyway. It'll be jammed by now, in the holidays. I haven't been doing anything."

They were going to the zoo. It was one of Hugh's favourite places. He went there often, by himself. He went to observe and also draw, animals, buildings, people – observing perhaps quite as much if not more than he actually drew, keeping all forms, animate or inanimate, in his head, playing around with them, distorting, rethinking them, and setting them on paper at last, if he ever did, transformed by his feelings and impressions; forms both remembered and remade.

These expeditions, however, were not only strictly solitary, but usually as early in the morning as the zoo opened. He had been planning this trip alone too – attracted as much as repelled by the prospect of the crowds, because he had meant to observe them as closely as he observed the animals – but his mother had seized on it as a means of paying back yesterday's hospitality by Penn's parents. (Penn's mother had given them all supper after the tournament.) Hugh had protested, of course, but less than he would have done ordinarily, because his wish to be solitary had been partly overlaid by the compulsion to be with the other three. He had no choice in any case. The matter was decided by his mother, which for once made things easier. She gave Hugh money for all of them and a picnic lunch, rather untidily wrapped. She also gave him three letters to post, because she said she would like them to have the zoo postmark on.

Penn had been angry about the zoo at first; he considered it childish. But he could offer no better suggestion, and when it came to it, all four being in a curiously dreamlike state that day, the zoo seemed as good a place to dream as anywhere. Even the ordinary animals seemed creatures of fantasy, and the stranger ones had never appeared so extraordinary: elongations, distortions, incredibilities; long-necked giraffes and long-nosed elephants, loose-limbed gibbons swinging hand over hand from rail to rail to rail, seals sliding into and through the water, smooth-skinned, rubbery (they barked and splashed, but the movements were unrelated, entirely silent); striped tigers; and lions, *lions*, thought Hugh, and pushed the thought of lions away, deliberately.

He went to the elephant house. House felt the wrong word though; it was more like being underground in an eccentrically lit and hewn-out cave, or like the crypt of a castle. (Hugh wished he could stop thinking of castles, too.) There were staged areas of orange light, in which framed by pillars, wrinkled, primaeval-looking creatures stood, elephants and rhinoceroses, their every wrinkle having definition and importance. Hugh felt as if he had never properly looked at either animal before. They were dusted most of them with yellow sand, this thicker in the cracks and wrinkles, and looked more like reptiles than animals with their naked skins and little, sunken eyes. They looked like that pig, Hugh thought, and again wished that he had not.

He stood and stared at one rhinoceros, bigger than the rest; it stared back with surprisingly mild-looking eyes, almost benevolent.

"Wouldn't like him for breakfast," a girl said behind Hugh and giggled. Hugh did not turn round, but glowered to himself.

There was a trench between animals and onlookers, a shallow trench with steps down into it and short stone blocks lining the centre, like old-fashioned milestones. It was scarcely a barrier. He and the rhinoceros might have been in the same dimension, there seemed nothing to stop Hugh reaching it, or it reaching him. It felt familiar suddenly, and then Hugh realised that it was like standing on the hill looking across at the castle. As then, he seemed close and yet remote. When there came sudden movement, he even expected it to be the man on horseback, but it was only a little girl who ran down from the viewing floor and clutched at one of the stone blocks in the trench. Hugh gasped, moved to snatch her from danger, his sense of alarm heightened by what he had been imagining. But no one else seemed to think it dangerous. A man walked down the steps and brought the child back on his shoulders, smiling, while behind him the rhinoceros ambled to the rear of its enclosure. It moved joint by joint as if made by an armourer. Its skin looked as if laid on it in plates, by nails. It did not look real at all, Hugh thought. Perhaps what seemed ordinary reality was no less odd than his new world after all, just as the new world could come to seem as ordinary as reality.

The other three waited outside the house.

"We've had enough of this. Let's eat in the park," said Penn.

"We could row on the lake then, afterwards," said Hugh, glad at the thought of escape, "I've got enough money left."

"The letters," Jean said. "Will you post them, Hugh?"

Hugh stood staring at the letters, blinking furiously, his eyes taking an inordinate time to adjust themselves to daylight.

"What's the matter?" asked Penn, echoed by Jean. All of them were staring at him oddly, Hugh thought. He glanced around wildly, he wanted to escape, but he could not; anywhere he turned he saw them, castles. The elephant house, the bear terraces, the seal rocks all looked rugged, turreted, like castles with battlements and towers.

He held up each of the letters in turn. There had been a new issue of stamps only yesterday. Hugh had never seen these before. One letter bore a stamp to go to America, another a fivepenny, the third a threepenny stamp. The theme was the castles of England: the first had Carmarthen Castle, the second Windsor, the third, Harlech Castle.

"Castles," Hugh said to himself, and then out loud

"Castles." He managed to shift himself and set off running through the crowds to find the postbox at the main gate. He could not get rid of the letters fast enough, they felt like fires in his hand, imagined or real he could not judge by now. He went to the wrong gate, and so could not find the postbox at first, dodging frantically through the milling and purpose-less crowd, mistaking a woman in red for the box once, and finding it at last more by luck than decision, throwing the letters in immediately. One missed the slot, it dropped, he had to pick it up again. And when it was done, when all three were gone, he leaned against the box, gasping, to the surprise of the postman who came at that moment to empty it.

"You all right, mate? You a student then? You've got the student look."

Hugh shook his head, and walked away soberly. His panic worked through him; slowly cooled, uncoiled itself. He took in the ordinary zoo for almost the first time that day, the sour smells of animal and chip fat and DDT: how hot it was and how hopelessly crowded. There were queues for every-thing, lavatories, snackbars, camel rides. Thousands of children in their best clothes ran around freely, but increas-ingly fractious, while animals prowled behind bars or ditches, or lay stretched, panting, in the heat of the sun.

CHAPTER 10

ANNA and Hugh shared one boat; Jean and Penn another. Anna very slowly and deliberately climbed into a boat with Hugh, Penn visibly annoyed by this, Jean upset because Penn was annoyed at having to share with her. Her way of demonstrating it was to be sharp and bossy, organising her face into a smile sometimes, but wasting it only on the water.

Penn demonstrated his annoyance by showing off wildly. He climbed to his feet, stood on the thwart, balancing precariously. Jean stopped smiling altogether, said "Don't, Penn," anxiously, first on his account and then on her own, as the boat swayed dangerously.

The boatman bellowed at them from his landing stage, threatening to fetch them in at once. Everyone rowing on the lake, the people walking along the shore, turned to look at them, making Jean blush scarlet. Penn muttered rudely, nothing that the boatman could have heard, sat down and began to row with furious but quite elegant efficiency, making the boat shoot through the water. He kept his eye triumphantly on Hugh struggling more clumsily at his oars behind, but though Hugh glanced round occasionally and coolly admired Penn's skill, Anna ignored him, trailed her hand in the water, turned her eyes towards the sky. She smiled at Hugh when he looked her way, but he tried not to do it often. He found her somehow embarrassing. Often he liked to cut himself off mentally from everyone around him, usually annoying people thus, but he could not now quite cut himself off from Anna, which at this moment only annoyed him. He avoided her eyes. She was holding hands with her-

64

self again, and she wore as usual a dark-coloured dress. But today it did not overshadow her.

Penn rowed so much faster that they lost him soon, round an island in the lake. Hugh rowed on towards the island. The branches of weeping willow brushed his face and shoulders like bead curtaining. He pushed them gently out of his way. He had stopped rowing now, but the impetus of movement already gained took them as far as he wanted, between the outer branches and the shores of the island. They slid through still water and came to a halt within a green cave.

Anna appeared to be asleep now. Hugh looked at her, then gingerly, carefully, laid himself back. The position he came to might, indeed should have been, uncomfortable, but was not so at all. He seemed automatically, without experiment, to have found a position into which every part of him neatly fitted, rested comfortably. He lay in contentment, gazing at a green ceiling. His hands and face were green-tinted, Anna's too, but green differentially. Here and there pure sun fell through the willow fronds. Hugh was so comfortable now that he could forget specific bones, specific physical sensations. He and the shade and the tree and the sun were all one and the same, all melting together. It was a cool, detached, thinking place, Hugh felt. The words "Green thought in a green shade" came from somewhere, he did not know where. He could think green, cool thoughts about castles; about the castle, about the cupboard, green, calm thoughts, compared to his panic that morning. It was as if he had fought in a vast wind then, but now the wind had died. He found himself contented, not at all afraid.

Anna sat up. Hugh felt her first in the rocking of the boat, and when he sat up himself found her gazing over the side of it. The water was very green and thick, her reflection green and remote and strange. She stirred the water with her finger, the image of her face shivered, disappeared, came together, her hand pausing, then disappeared again. The small ebbs of water caught points of light that Hugh would not have known existed in this shade.

Hugh wanted to reach, if not Anna herself, the image of Anna. Beyond, infinitely deep, as the water shivered and before it settled he seemed to see another image, of a castle, and he wanted to reach that too. He realised he wanted to think of it, to be reminded of it. He wanted terribly to reach it. But the water stilled, the castle was not there.

"The water's filthy," Anna said.

"It's a beautiful colour," Hugh said.

"It looks like soup. It ought to smell horrible."

"But it doesn't," Hugh said.

"It doesn't smell nice, either."

There was further silence. Hugh had no inclination to break it, but after a few minutes Anna said: "I was thinking about the cupboard; your cupboard."

"Just for once I wasn't," Hugh said.

"What do you think, when you do think?"

"How should I know now?" Hugh did not want to commit himself.

"You must know!"

"Nothing useful, anyway." But suddenly Hugh did want to tell Anna about the castle, everything. It was as if a space had opened in him, revealed something he did not know was there. The wanting sprang at him from nothing, but the desire fought inability. He could not tell her, could not find the means. Words framed themselves only to split upon his tongue. She did not seem to want to be told in any case. Every time he thought he had gathered himself to speak, she ran her fingers roughly through the water, or shook her head, or turned abruptly, or said something herself about ducks, the tree, the zoo, always something trivial, if not downright silly, or at least it might have been downright silly, or she might have deliberately calculated silliness. Hugh by now would not have put that past her. Eventually he told her just about his experiments that morning, timing the brass buttons, though he missed out his wanting to get into the cupboard.

Anna was still silent when he finished. Hugh watched her reflection in the water with almost the same curious nostalgia he had felt for the girl in the alder grove; both girl and reflection thankfully unobtainable.

"Would your old man be able to explain us anything?" asked Anna startling him. "The one in the shop, you said."

"We could try I suppose."

"Then go and ask him. If you want to know."

"Do you want to know? But what do I say. Er um did you know you'd sold me a magic cupboard, sir?"

"That's *your* problem not mine," said Anna calmly. "Now listen, if someone got into the cupboard, they might be made younger, mightn't they, just like Penn said?"

"We thought of that yesterday."

"I thought of it, you mean." But Hugh wanted to think about this even less than he had wanted to think about the old man, because of what had happened this morning.

"Anyone old could get into the cupboard and be made young again. They could grow old again and be made young again. They needn't ever die."

"I suppose they wouldn't. But think of the practical problems."

"They would be immortal," Anna said.

"An odd sort of immortality. Gods are immortal, but they always stay the same. They don't ever get old, get young again."

"I'd hate that," Anna said.

"Some people don't want to be made immortal at all. Odysseus didn't. We read the Odyssey at school last term. You know, Odysseus. Ulysses."

"Ulysses. I know," said Anna, nodding. "Why didn't he?"

"There was something about him just wanting to be alive, the master said."

"I don't understand that."

"I didn't understand it either."

"I'd like to be immortal if I could go on changing," said Anna. "But I think I'd have to go on changing."

"Some Indian religions say you change totally. After death you come back to life as an animal, insect, anything. I read that once."

"That's silly. You know it's not what I meant."

"I'd be a bird, I think, if I was allowed to choose."

"I'd be a squirrel or a monkey. I'd like to leap and swing, like those gibbons in the zoo."

"That's flying too, of a sort," Hugh said. "Would you really want to be made young, Anna, over and over again, and grow old again. To change and change for ever and for ever?"

"I change anyway. I change every day, don't you? I feel years older than Jean. Sometimes I feel years older than you." Anna was laughing at him suddenly.

"You surprise me. Anyone would think you were Methuselah. You look ancient, I must say, Anna. Come off it, for heaven's sake."

"Come off what?" asked another voice. It was Penn this time, holding aside the trailing branches, letting in a swathe of light and sun, a view of the world outside. Hugh did not want it, world or light or Penn. He felt a sudden total fury.

But Penn stood in the bows of his boat like a figurehead, triumphant, all his ill-humour gone; perhaps it had been transferred to Jean, who looked, behind him, red-faced and annoyed.

"He won't let me row, Hugh. He hasn't let me row at all."

Penn laughed at her. "She is entirely in my power. If she snatches at the oars she'll just upset the boat."

"Hugh, he's horrible, it isn't fair. Can't I come with you, you'd let me row."

"Willingly," Hugh answered lazily. It was as if a switch had flicked, his fury gone utterly, he could not remember what it felt like. "I hate rowing myself." But he found when he came to it that he was less happy to relinquish his companion. He would rather have rowed with Anna or with Penn than Jean, who moved into his boat clumsily, not rocking it too much, but still much less neat than Anna, who smiled gently as she sat herself down in Penn's boat.

Their hour was almost up. Penn rowed off at full speed, widening the gap between their boats at every stroke. Anna sat in the stern with her back to Hugh and Jean. Her voice and Penn's floated across the water, but Hugh could not hear anything that was said. Jean's rowing was perfectly adequate, but she kept up a running commentary on the techniques involved that he did not feel in the least like listening to. She fell silent at last out of weariness; but Hugh did not offer to take over the oars. Aware, without guilt, that he was being mean, he lay with his hands behind his head and simply enjoyed himself again, let the sun, the slight wind, the cool movement of water calm him, just as he had been calmed earlier in the green willow cave.

CHAPTER 11

THEY went home as they had come, by bus and underground. In the tunnels, in the dark, the distances seemed interminable if you once began to count. But when the train broke out into the light, when the eye had something it could reckon by, even twice the distance might seem half the length. So time always was in part what you made of it, Hugh thought, a little comforted. It made the cupboard seem a shade less ruthless, a shade less arbitrary.

They walked in at the front gate, hot and cross after the walk from the station.

"Where's Humbert?" Jean asked at once. Humbert was the cat, Jean's in effect, because no one else took much notice of him, except occasionally their father who fondled him extravagantly before visitors, or when he felt some kind of need to show affection. In the summer, in the heat, Humbert's favourite place was beneath the ash tree in the front garden, – he had been sitting there when they went out, but was not on their return.

"He'll be somewhere. He could be anywhere. You know what cats are like."

It was odd that Jean worried so very soon. But when they did begin to look for him he was nowhere to be found. His dish of food had not been touched either.

Jean was beside herself. She seemed at the moment too easily upset, who was normally quite calm and organised. She went all round the house, all round the garden, calling quietly, "Puss, puss, puss." To no avail; by bedtime she was crying unashamedly.

"We shouldn't have gone out. We shouldn't have left him. It's all our fault."

"Don't be silly; Ma was here." And they'd often left him, Hugh pointed out, gently. He'd often gone off and then come back. Cats were like that, independent, solitary. "I'm dead sympathetic to cats," Hugh said with feeling; remembering he'd hardly been left alone to paint for a week, and wishing, almost, that the cupboard had never happened.

He went upstairs to bed still thinking of painting, not thinking about the cupboard at all. But there had been a tree in his most recent painting, somewhat abstract but a tree for all that, dominating it, and it was a tree he began to feel as he neared his room; an ash tree, he decided, because that was where they'd last seen the cat. He expected the cupboard to be a tree, to have taken root, to be growing in his room. He opened the door quite sure of that, to find only the ordinary shoddy-looking cupboard, marked by nails where there had been a mirror, and the ash tree as usual outside his window. Yet he had imagined an ash tree in his room, with a smooth trunk and sprays of little leaves.

His mind kept on going back to it. Lying in bed he found himself in a boat, floating beneath the shade of a huge ash tree. Tonight he felt wholly as if in a dream. A boatman stood in the bows of the boat and poled it with a long grey pole. Hugh could not see the boatman's face, but this did not worry him – he seemed to know everything, somewhere in his mind.

The castle lay ahead of them across the lake. Hugh looked for and found its reflection in the water, but under the lake he saw another world again, the castle surrounded by flowing grass and trees, trees with fruit on them and some with flowers, all greenish-tinged, all the other colours there but subordinate. Hugh longed for the castle, stretched out his hands to its reflection, the boat gentling and gliding under him. His hands touched the water, stirring it, and ripples came and broke the world. Then he awoke to lie quite calm and peaceful, his body, released, almost floating in the bed. He did not need to move to make himself comfortable. He fell asleep like that and did not dream and woke in the morning lying as before, not a limb having shifted, not a finger.

It was very early, well before breakfast. Hugh got up and went to the park and walked by himself in clear, cool sunlight; shadows important, light significant. Sight and sound were quite separate experiences – the roads were full of cars taking people to work, but the noise they made was not at all related to the engines that made it. It was a calm, a whole, yet disjointed world, empty of anyone save Hugh himself. The people in cars were part of the machines and so did not count, he thought, as people.

He walked for much longer than he meant and came back late even for his mother's breakfast, meeting Penn and Anna at the gate. Both looked cross, appeared to be arguing – they stopped when Hugh arrived and smiled at him, but the smiles might have been to spite each other rather than welcome him, he thought.

The house smelt of sausages and shaving soap, among other familiar things harder to define because they were always there and well amalgamated. But as they went down the basement stairs, another smell met them, strong, unpleasant, all too recognisable.

"Cat," said Penn, disapprovingly.

"But our cat . . ." said Hugh.

"Perhaps Humbert's come back," Anna said.

But there was in the kitchen no full-grown Humbert,

only a black kitten regarding gingerly a saucerful of milk. On the other side of the saucer Jean knelt, looking at the kitten.

"He's sweet," she said. "He was sitting outside the cat door, just as if he wanted to come in."

"He's peed. It stinks," Penn said.

"Perhaps we could keep him even if Humbert does come back. He looks a bit like Humbert . . ."

"Black all over," Anna said.

The moment he had seen the kitten Hugh knew what had happened; what the kitten was. Anna knew too. He looked at her quickly, found her looking at him – both hastily removed their eyes from each other. Anna scratched her nose and chewed her tongue and seemed not particularly concerned. Hugh, decidedly shaken, looked at the table and considered unenthusiastically a cold sausage and two elderly slices of toast.

"Is that my breakfast? Where's Ma?"

"Upstairs, cross, gone to get you out of bed."

"I've been for a walk. God almighty, we usually have to get *her* up," said Hugh indignantly.

"She was in that sort of mood this morning. You know, energetic."

"For once," said Hugh.

"Your ma *energetic?*" Penn asked.

"Shut up," said Hugh furiously. "It's none of your business."

"Isn't your room still in a mess?" asked Jean.

The kitten was actually lapping now; lapping milk slowly, with deliberation.

"Humbert," Hugh said. And felt Anna nod.

"We can't call him Humbert. Humbert might come back. It's still only one night after all."

73

"He won't come back," said Hugh, but to himself.

Anna paused when they started up the stairs, waiting for Hugh who was scavenging for food.

"Do you remember what we said yesterday?" Hugh ate the end of a sausage and considered the question. He could see Penn looking down at them with some hostility.

"Immortality," hissed Anna eagerly.

"I don't think much of an immortal cat," said Hugh.

"The Egyptians thought cats were immortal, sacred anyway. We've got a postcard on our mantelpiece."

"What are you talking about. What's got into you, Ann?" shouted Penn from the top of the basement stairs.

"Nothing, except my brother," Anna said coldly.

They met Hugh's mother in the hall, still in her dressing-gown and very indignant. All the time she was shouting she looked at Hugh's toast and marmalade, as if wondering whether to eat a slice of it herself.

"Why can't you have your breakfast at the same time as everyone else?"

"There isn't a time in this house . . . Just because you woke up for once . . ."

She let it pass. It was his room she was really concerned about, working herself up into a greater and greater rage as she went along, having started relatively calm. She stood in the middle of the stairs, blocking the way up – Penn tried to dodge past her, but without seeming to notice she moved when he did, so preventing him.

Anna was giggling, a silly schoolgirl giggle, at Penn, annoying him, at Hugh's mother, annoying and confusing Hugh, who did not know which of them to turn on first, his mother for attacking him, or Anna for attacking his mother. His anger mounting, though undirected, he scarcely took in anything that was said, knew only that the abuse was centred on his room, its chaos. On the empty, apparently unused cupboard.

Shock was delayed when it came. Hugh heard the words clearly, but did not take them in. It was like this morning, seeing an action at a distance and hearing it fractionally later, except that this time it was the other way about. The sound came first; seconds later arrived the blow.

Penn's mouth was open. Hugh at first could not imagine why. Then he saw that Anna's expression was curious too, amused, perhaps triumphant, and yet alarmed.

Since Hugh had been so slow to put his clothes away, well she had done it for him, his mother had said.

"*Jesus,*" said Hugh those seconds later, diving past her, up the stairs. His mother's voice floated angrily after him, but he scarcely heard it, tearing breathlessly up the red-carpeted stairs, his step never matching the tread or two treads he was trying to take – too long, too short, his pace disjointed, the very fall of his feet knocking the breath from him. His mind seemed to burst with the dangers and possibilities.

"You won't have any clothes left for a start." Penn behind Hugh did not sound even out of breath. Anna appeared to be laughing; Jean puzzled, frightened, uncomprehending. "What's happened, someone tell me?" she went on and on, all the way upstairs, more and more breathlessly.

But when Hugh at last flung open the bedroom door there was nothing. The room looked much as he had left it earlier, his pyjamas on the floor, his bed unmade. The only difference was that some of the untidy piles of clothes had been removed from the chest-of-drawers and placed in still untidier piles on the cupboard shelves. But clothes they remained and nothing else. For his mother, typically, had failed to shut the door. Pants, vests and shirts, were still pants, vests and shirts, not collections of miscellaneous materials or blundering frightened animals.

Hugh and Penn collapsed simultaneously, laughing, and rolled together across the floor, punching each other, laughing again and punching again, to the ribs or face or chest, punches not serious, scarcely felt, shadow-boxing like young animals.

But when they stopped, as suddenly as they had begun, climbing to their feet, dusting each other down, Hugh saw Anna by the window, unsmiling.

"Come on, better get this lot cleared up a bit," said Penn officiously. "Come on, Anna, get moving, girl."

But she did not move. She did not seem to hear. For the first time Hugh began to take it in, the atmosphere here, in the room.

Outside, the clarity and glitter of the early morning had vanished. The sky had not so much clouded over as thickened to a grey haze, not dark but sullen, emphasising the heaviness of late summer foliage, its lack of bloom and life. Hugh imagined autumn with relief.

But it was more than that. Outside the ash tree blocked the window and there was a constant procession of holiday aircraft, flying low because of the haze, the haze itself trapping in the roar of their engines, bringing it right into the room, thunderous, oppressive, heavy. Yet the centre of the power that oppressed Hugh so utterly came from within the room itself. It came from the cupboard; engulfing, enormous and quite impersonal, so that Penn's efficient activity taking clothes from shelves and hangers seemed merely busy and insignificant. The black kitten strolling into the room, its tail pointing to the ceiling, looked more important, curiously. Yet it was ridiculously small.

Jean fell on the kitten with relief, but it twisted from her hands and settled calmly by the window, with all the assurance and indifference of an adult cat.

"I wonder where Humbert is," said Jean.

"This is Humbert."

"A kitten. Don't be idiotic, Ann."

"It *can't* be Humbert." Jean did not even want to believe it.

"It is Humbert, isn't it, Hugh? Hugh and I talked about it yesterday. This sort of thing."

"Why didn't you talk to me?" asked Penn.

"You wouldn't have listened. You're pig-headed, Penn. You tell him, Hugh."

Hugh reluctantly tried to explain, but it was difficult, Penn intrigued but not wanting to believe out of pride, and Jean not wanting to believe out of fear. Anna's self-righteous look made Hugh wish he could disbelieve it himself, but in the face of the black kitten's presence and the mysterious and unprecedented absence of the black Humbert, the explanation did seem all too probable.

"He must have got into the cupboard while we were out yesterday."

"But how could he have shut the door?"

"Well that is a bit odd, I know," admitted Hugh, but it did not affect his certainty.

"It turned other things back, didn't it?" Anna pressed; the harder it was to disbelieve her, the angrier Penn grew.

"We'll have to shove you in to make sure, Ann."

"Oh no *you*, Penn. You were such a sweet little boy, everybody said."

"Well you looked like the back end of a bus. So everybody said."

"You were so pretty, you looked just like a girl."

The angrier Penn got, the sillier the insults; Hugh had

hardly seen him so angry before. He started throwing clothes on to the bed, furiously, as if they were weapons. His anger made him powerful, almost as powerful as the cupboard itself, but the fury appeared to bounce off Anna. She stood calmly watching him in the middle of the room.

"I can show you. Ma has those photographs of when you were little. I'll show you the one of Penn without any clothes on, Hugh. He looked sweet." Anna's voice rose. "Suppose we put him in the cupboard and he came out like that?"

Hugh and Jean might have been in a different world. Watching Penn and watching Anna, Hugh felt wholly remote from them. He could look away, and it would not be happening. It was like a picture flickering on a screen that you could turn off with a switch. Only there was no switch, and he could not look away, and it went on happening.

"You'd be much much nicer, Penn. I could cuddle you."

Anna was no longer cool, but laughing, a little hysterically. And when Penn, the cupboard emptied, turned on her, lashing out blindly, she took the excuse to lose her temper too. Penn lashing out, she jumped at him. Penn stepped back from her, and taken off balance lurched, stepped back again, swayed awkwardly and fell into the cupboard. It was almost as if, voluntarily, he folded himself up in it, because Anna was able to slam the doors on him. Hugh would have expected the furious Penn to push them open instantly, but he did not. The cupboard remained shut.

It was so sudden. First this had not happened, then it had. Anna covered her face, looking small, thin, childish. She took her hands away and stared helplessly at Hugh, horrified, yet dazed as if she had suddenly woken from a sleep. She stood alone beside the cupboard door, but it was Hugh who took the four long, creaking steps across the room and opened it, noticing as he did so his sister Jean, mouth open, eyes open, totally startled, almost a caricature of surprise, like someone drawn in a comic strip.

He stood, holding open the cupboard door. His eyes descended. Looking at first for the boy Penn, his vision had to adjust itself to the proper scale, to find at last no Penn he knew, but a baby in T-shirt and dungarees, with reddish curly hair, holding a brass button out to him and smiling unconcernedly.

He was so nice, that was the trouble. For it only made this still more horrible.

CHAPTER 12

"It can't be Penn. It can't be." Jean's voice shook miserably. The baby waved his arms up and down, giggled, and crawled out of the cupboard.

Hugh dragged his mind back, tried to force the presence of this baby towards the earlier presence of Penn, to make himself understand properly that this could be Penn.

"Who else could it be?" He spoke aloud to convince himself.

"We must put him back in the cupboard quickly. Quickly."

"Don't be stupid. What good would that do?" Hugh felt weary. A lethargy came over him at the thought of trying to resolve this, at the thought that he had to, Penn having left him to decide alone.

A wave of furious anger came over him as well that Penn should have so abandoned him. He touched a chair, could have thrown it across the room, but the anger faded, left him void and cold.

"What are we going to do?" he said.

"Look after him, obviously." The immediate and pressing practical problems began to have the effect of calming Jean. When the baby, crawling for a chair, almost pulled it down upon his head and began to wail, she moved quickly, picked him up, cuddled him, murmuring.

"Shut him up *quick*," Hugh said. "Or Ma will hear."

"What if she does come?"

"We'll hear her. We'll have to hide him fast."

"Hide a *baby*. Are you *joking?*"

"She mustn't know."

"But someone's bound to notice Penn's missing, some time."

The baby was quiet now, patting at Jean's cheek. Jean shifted her face to one side of him to look at Anna. Hugh looked too, almost simultaneously. Anna was standing quite still, her arms by her sides, with hands curled up, shaking all over. Her eyes were shut, tears were spilling out and pouring down her cheeks.

"Anna," Hugh said, questioningly. "Anna?"

She opened her eyes and looked at him.

"It's done now. It's happened. I think," he said cautiously, "it would have happened some time anyway." But the tears continued pouring down Anna's face.

"You will have to pull yourself together, Anna," said Jean officiously, who had herself panicked so thoroughly earlier. The baby was pulling at her hair now.

"Tonight's all right," she added. "Penn and Anna are meant to be staying with us tonight anyway or they could if they wanted to, Mum said. Their mother's going out."

"But . . ." Hugh made a helpless, hopeless gesture. Anna merely began to weep out loud. Hugh wanted to go away now, do nothing, seek no solutions, but pulled himself out of that, through irritation mostly.

"Shut *up*, Jean. It's all right, Anna."

"It isn't all right. How can we get him *back?*" Anna's voice wailed somewhat, but at least she began to look more normal. For an unpleasant moment Hugh had wondered if she might be going to faint; she had looked so ashen white.

"I don't know, not yet. We'll think of something. But I don't know, *yet*."

The baby had started whimpering. Jean looked helpless again. "Do you suppose he's hungry?" She jigged him up and down, but to little avail. Anna walked across the room and looked into the baby's face as it peered over Jean's shoulder.

"He *is* Penn. He looks like Penn." The baby stopped whimpering and stared at her for a long time, solemnly. Then suddenly he smiled, while Anna smiled back. Hugh had never seen her smile like that before. It was a nice smile apart from anything else, and he realised he did not always like Anna very much, that is he did not always think her nice.

Both Anna and Jean seemed after a little while to become more concerned by the immediate problems of child-minding than by anything else. Hugh envied them.

"How old do you suppose he is?"

"Fourteen months? Sixteen?" Jean hazarded.

"What do babies of sixteen months eat, then?"

"Chopped things."

"Liver, I remember," said Anna. "Oh and mince. My aunt gave her baby mince once, I saw."

"But not raw mince. And we can't cook. Not without questions."

"How long is he going to stay like this? For goodness *sake*," Anna sounded frantic again, but this was a point that none of them cared to contemplate for the moment, and Jean suggested hastily, "There are always those little jars. You know the ones."

"Yes, but those are for little, *tiny* babies."

"There are some for bigger babies too. Chopped things."

"Well, give him those then." Hugh was bored of the discussion by now. "And meantime keep an eye on him. An eye . . ." He made a dive. The infant had started wriggling frantically. He was heavy enough, hard enough to hold without that, so Jean had been forced to set him down, and in the discussion they had all forgotten him. Now Hugh saw him put the flex of the record player in his mouth. "Jesus, he'll kill himself," he said. But the flex taken away from him, Penn howled and struggled in Hugh's unpractised arms.

"Shut him *up*, Hugh. Everyone will hear. For goodness *sake*."

"Shut him up yourself if you're so clever. Look, we'll have to get a room organised for him. Your room's better," Hugh added hastily.

"My room isn't so lethal. It had better be mine. I'll clear it up with Anna. You can get the baby food, Hugh."

"I can do *what?*" Hugh was appalled. "I haven't any money . . ." Then, realising it was a chance to escape if only for a short while, added, "I dare say I could raise some."

Outside the house the ordinariness of things was astonishing, but equally so was the far from ordinary way in which Hugh found himself observing them. It felt a little like coming out of an exhibition of modern paintings, when the whole familiar world looks different, strange, as if recomposed or reinterpreted by a particular artist, as if you looked at everything through his eyes. Or it felt like looking through a mirror into a familiar room, seeing familiar objects, yet in an unfamiliar dimension. Hugh – or rather his mirrored image – belonged to and yet was cut off from this world. It looked at once familiar yet wholly strange.

There was no traffic for the moment, and silence lay around him, a grey woolly kind of silence, though voices and feet were clear – the two girls walking on the far side of the road might have been next to Hugh on the same pavement. It was not like being outside at all, Hugh thought. He felt as if he was indoors, shut in a closed room. The sky was a ceiling, not space and infinite, it shut him in and offered no escape.

The silence was broken by a procession of hearses returning to the undertaker's down the hill. (Dead weddings, Jean had called funerals when she was small, Hugh remembered, wondering what ceremony or ritual you could invent to encompass what had happened to Penn.) Each sound seemed clear, unrelated to other sounds. Everything Hugh saw now also had a clarity, a curious definition; a tree, a fence, even a paving stone, seemed to exist in a world containing only itself, a world that sucked Hugh in as he looked at it. He had literally to drag his gaze away each time.

So it was with the racks of baby food in the chemist's shop. They made decidedly a separate world, one quite alien to him. Hugh had never noticed them before except as part of the décor of the chemist's shop, but now nothing might have existed for him but the possibilities of beef with tomatoes, or veal with rice, or lamb with vegetables, all sealed in jars with coloured labels on. For anything he knew, he had gazed at them for hours, equally he might have started only a minute or so ago. He did not know at all.

"Can I help you?" a voice asked loudly. Hugh jumped, and also, to his annoyance, blushed slightly. "I want some of these," he said, and blurted – to his annoyance once again – "for my younger brother."

"I never thought it was for you. Well, take your time then. Looking's free, unlike most things." The assistant was very young, but Hugh did not look long enough to know much more than that, whether she was as pretty as she was impertinent. Annoyed with both her and himself, he became decisive, took a jar of spaghetti with beef, another of vegetables with lamb, a third of pears with apple; but a fourth – chocolate custard – he had to replace hastily, realising he had enough money only for three. That cleaned him out, as it was, for the rest of the week. Hugh hoped Jean had some money, or Anna, whose brother after all was causing the expense, and wondered disconsolately again how long this could possibly go on.

A very old man came into the shop just as Hugh was leaving it and asked for cough lozenges. His voice was like the shadow of a voice, the frail centre, from which the rest, the resonance, had been honed away. His clothes hung as on a frame. His face was suspended between two great ears and a jutting nose; two noses would have seemed appropriate for total symmetry. Hugh, half out of the shop already, stopped still and stared at him.

At first he thought: I'd rather die before I become as old as that. And then he wondered what would the old man have looked like young and then what would happen to him if he was put into the cupboard. Would he be made young also? Or could someone be too old for the cupboard to change them? And how much younger would he be made if the cupboard did work? A middle-aged man – a young man – a baby? The thought of him as a baby was bizarre – or bizarre looked at conventionally. But Hugh could feel normality slipping away, the fixed world melting about him. Who would look after him if he became a baby? He would not be claimed by anyone, his real parents must have died generations ago. Would you wrap him in newspaper and leave him on a doorstep, like the cases reported in the evening newspapers? Or would you be able at once to find someone who wanted a baby to adopt? All these odd possibilities and practical dilemmas merged in Hugh's mind and moved it on elsewhere to another old man – the old man in the junk shop. What he had to do with the cupboard. Was it merely in his shop by chance? The thoughts galloped through Hugh's head, a succession partly verbal and partly visual. Which was which he could not have said, except for one vivid picture of a baby on a doorstep and the door opening upon it. Nor could he have told how long they lasted, but the old man still had his hand out for lozenges, when the assistant said, "Did they never tell you it's rude to stare? Perhaps you've a little sister too. How about buying her some baby soap?"

"No thank you," Hugh said coldly, and walked out of the shop very slowly and deliberately. But then he ran, all the way home, clutching the bag that held the jars of baby food, and bumped into his mother at the front gate.

"I did tell Jean. I'm going out. There's cheese and eggs, you know, when you want lunch. Oh and lots of yoghourt."

"There's always yoghourt," Hugh said. "The last lot was there so long it was bad when I wanted it."

"And salad. Jean can make a salad as well as I can."

"Better," muttered Hugh, which was not, he knew, strictly fair, because one thing his mother not only did, but could do, was cook, if she did tend to eat half her ingredients in the process.

"You're going out? *Where?*" asked Hugh – not because he wanted to know really, or even minded if he did not; yet he felt, obscurely, that he had a right to know.

She did not answer. At once, after all, he minded very much.

He asked again, "Where are you going to?"

"Penn and Anna can stay if they want."

"Why don't you ever listen," said Hugh, "when I ask you anything?"

"And of course they may be staying tonight in any case. Penn and Anna, Hugh."

"I wasn't asking about them."

"Why shouldn't they stay to lunch too? There's plenty of yoghourt."

"They'd better like yoghourt." The baby might eat it, Hugh thought. That meant they could save the jar of apples and pears till tomorrow. Tomorrow. His mind tried to shy away from that word, but only came back to it. Tomorrow and tomorrow and tomorrow ran through his mind. They had been reading Macbeth at school last term. Macbeth's problems, he thought bitterly, had nothing whatever on his, murder was *nothing* by comparison with this.

Then it dawned on him that with his mother gone, they would be safe for a while at least. It was very odd, he thought, that it had taken him all this time to realise it. Now he was impatient for her to go. He saw her look down at his hands, at the bag of baby foods, carried half open, carelessly. But she did not seem to take in its contents and he closed it hastily.

"You might wash up. I'll be back by three. I'm only shopping."

Four, with luck, that meant, thought Hugh. She leant forward suddenly, might have been about to kiss him, but withdrew. There was a hole in the armpit of her shirt. She went straight off and up the road.

"Why are you buying *baby* food?" she called back suddenly, but did not wait for an answer. Hugh felt almost faint with shock. He dropped the bag and had to pick it up again. The glass jars, fortunately, remained intact.

His mother might just as well have been in a glass jar too, he thought, or himself for that matter (but he had a sudden image of the nameless horrid things kept in jars in the school laboratory). They might have been mouthing at each other in mirrors, seeing images similar, but different from themselves.

Upstairs Hugh felt as much outside of things. The girls' fussing over Penn excluded him; he did not know whether he cared or not, decided probably not. Jean's room had been turned effectively into a nursery. She had improvised a cot with the mattress that was kept jammed under her bed and had been for years, and which was brought out whenever she or Hugh had friends to stay. Indeed either Penn or Anna would have slept on it tonight. But now she had put it in a corner and fenced it around with chairs. "I shouldn't think he could get out of that," she said. She had also dug out a whole lot of toys from somewhere, mostly very battered.

"Isn't it a good thing your mother doesn't throw things away," Anna observed.

"The garden shed's just full of marvellous things," said Jean enthusiastically – she had even found an ancient pushchair. Hugh had to help the girls set it up, for it had been folded so long it was reluctant to unfold at all; its joints seemed set, its parts inseparable. Nor were they assisted by having the infant Penn crawling about their feet, and by the kitten which had elected to appear from the basement, pleased with itself for some reason, purring loudly, and insinuating itself among them, until Hugh trod on a paw by accident, whereupon it miauled indignantly and retired to a safer distance.

Eventually, the three of them pulling as hard as they could, the pushchair unfolded, clicked into shape. It was a little drunken-looking perhaps and decidedly rusty; but a useable pushchair for all that.

"Penn could have done that on his own. He's strong enough," said Anna.

"Well, Penn's not here, is he?" said Hugh, the unkindness affecting himself as much as Anna.

"Why do you want the pushchair?" he suddenly inquired. "Surely you're not going to take him out?"

"No one will know who he is," said Jean. "We'll just say we're obliging someone, looking after him."

"You're *mad*," said Hugh. "We don't know anyone with kids that age."

"If we just take him in the garden there'll be questions anyway," said Jean.

"If we take him out," said Anna, "he's more likely to get to sleep."

The baby fell asleep after they had fed it, to their relief. It was perhaps only then that they realised quite how much he worried them – they might have been living with a bomb that could explode at any time. They ate their lunch like people between air-raids, indeed it was a meal quite as haphazard as any such, Jean not bothering for once to organise at all. They sat on the kitchen table eating boiled eggs, damp lettuce straight out of the colander in which it had been washed, and hunks of bread and butter. No one touched the yoghourt, but they devoured almost a packet of sultanas, Hugh admittedly having the lion's share. He was thankful he had not had to eat the glutinous-looking strange mess that came out of the baby jars. Penn did not seem to have cared for it too much either, judging by the amount he had managed to spit out, with a delighted smile. In the end they had had to fill him up with cheese. Jean had said that she was sure babies should not have cheese, but Anna retorted that it was better than leaving him to wail with hunger, announcing his presence to everyone.

Hugh left the house on his own after lunch before Penn had woken, not saying that he was going, let alone where.

He thought: they wouldn't be interested anyway. They were only interested in Penn. He was halfway up the road before he knew where he was going himself, and then again he did not know if he had decided it himself or whether it had been decided for him. Either way there was no doubt. It was where he had to go.

He went down the hill, back to the junk shop, pushed the door, and went straight inside. The smell and the dim light were immediately wholly familiar. But when his eyes had accustomed themselves to the gloom, he saw that something else was different; more, very very different. He ought to have known why immediately. But it was as if he had seen the shop in a dream before. He could not visualise, merely summon up a feeling of what it had been like. Not until he deliberately stopped himself trying to remember and let impressions sweep over him unimpeded, did he realise what had happened. The shop was emptier, not just a little, much emptier. The furniture was still there, or a fair amount of it, blocks and forms and shadowy shapes, but most of the clutter had vanished from the surfaces and nothing hung from the ceiling now. There had been no tables outside the shop either, Hugh remembered suddenly, no boxes of books and junk and jewellery, and piles of 78-speed gramophone records. He wondered what had happened to everything. It could not, surely, have been sold in just a week.

The shock was as great as the first time; of coming from light into shadow, from warmth into chill. A whole chain of reactions seemed to be set off in him – first he noticed the difference, then at last he placed it, the relative emptiness; then he saw the blind head – on a table now, in a corner and without its wig; and then he saw the old man looming from a doorway.

"I was only looking," Hugh said, apologetically.

"Looking's free," observed the old man: at which Hugh, instantly, from nothing, wanted to laugh, an emotion puzzling to him, almost embarrassing, and quite inappropriate in these circumstances; but the pert girl in the chemist's had said exactly the same thing, and it seemed so out of place here, like a dirty limerick spoken in the school chapel. He stared at the old man defiantly. "I'll go on looking then," he said.

His eyes had adapted to the dimness now. He saw a single object on every single piece of furniture, or on a wall above, a whole range of objects, each one as separate and distinct as before they had been indistinguishable amid the general clutter; yet each one at the same time related to all the others, though how he could not say. There was the familiar yet still disconcerting blind head. There was a squat stone figure of a monk; an eighteenth-century miniature, a wooden oval disc with a face carved on it in relief – it should, he guessed, have hung upon a wall, but now lay face upwards on a marble stand – and another wooden head, more jutting and ornate, which might have been one of a pair supporting a doorhead or a mantelpiece. There was a group of pottery figures, a sailor, a girl, a curly-tailed dog, all brightly painted so far as it was possible to tell in this gloom; a medallion very tarnished which looked old – was it Roman, Hugh wondered. It had a face on it too, and so did the small chipped saucer on the table next to it, a formal portrait head. On the wall above these, equidistant from both, hung a little print of a man on horseback, etched or engraved, brown-spotted with damp.

Everything, every object had a face, Hugh realised, the

same face, one he half recognised, but could not place. The looking, however, so absorbed him that the voice from the inner doorway made him jump uncomfortably.

"You came with your father before, young man."

Hugh turned towards the voice, the shadowed face. "We bought a cupboard. Yes," he said.

"Ah yes. I remember it; a cupboard with qualities."

"Some qualities," Hugh said. "It was a very ugly cupboard too." For a moment he only remembered the ugliness of the cupboard and nothing else at all.

"You may call it ugly if you like."

"It *is* ugly. It's why I came. I came about your cupboard." Hugh spoke quietly. He had thought he would have to force himself to be calm, but it was not difficult at all. He felt calm and controlled and certain what he meant; at the same time cut off, separate from everything. "Your cupboard changes things," he said.

"It's your cupboard, not mine. You bought it from me. Or your father did. It is his cupboard, I should have thought. What did you expect? What was I supposed to offer you? Continuity? Security? Immunity? Immunity from what?"

"I don't know what you're talking about. If you buy a cupboard you don't expect it to change things. That's all." The words were protesting enough, but Hugh, feeling it entirely absurd that he had to protest at all, could not put much heat into his voice. All at once the whole thing seemed ridiculous. He was himself ridiculous. "It changes *people*," he said trying to retrieve the seriousness of the situation and yet somehow not able at this moment to feel serious enough, in spite of everything.

He wondered, suddenly, what Anna would have thought of him.

"It's not so unusual for people to change," said the old man, prim as a governess.

"Not like that they don't. What's it made of?" Hugh managed to sound a little more insistent; yet still, inappropriately, wanted to laugh.

"What would you have liked it to be made of? Gingerbread?" asked the old man. But now he turned and led Hugh out of the shop into his little back room, flicking a switch as he went, so that they passed from dimness to light again – which made Hugh blink uncomfortably. There was a bare bulb swinging idly on a long flex, throwing shadows of itself upon the walls. There was a table with papers on it, an unlit gas fire, an electric kettle, but, surprisingly, not a single chair or stool. The old man's face had turned to islands and shadows now.

"You should have warned us," Hugh said. "Why didn't you warn us?"

"Would you rather it had not changed things? You could have bought some other cupboard. Cupboards are not in short supply."

"It was the only cupboard in your shop, though," said Hugh. He avoided answering the real question. But the answer came rushing at him even so, and he resented this answer because the cupboard had been, to say the least of it, inconvenient, upsetting everything he had meant to do, destroying his solitude, stopping his painting, imposing impossible problems on him, and leaving him to solve them without Penn, alone.

"I might be glad in a way," he said angrily. Then laughed out loud. "It's all right for Penn. He can't notice anything, he doesn't have to do anything. He just has to be looked after. Jesus, I wish it had happened to me, not Penn."

"You have a different role," the old man said.

"Then you do know about it?" But the old man looked at him and shook his head very slightly. They stood in silence for a while. "What's the cupboard made of?" Hugh asked. The old man went past him back into the shop and fetched a chair, but neither of them sat down on it. They continued to stand beneath the naked, swinging bulb, which went on swinging for reasons of its own, making little reflections of the room and them.

"What shall we do? How can we get Penn back?"

"The cupboard is made of apple wood," said the old man slowly and deliberately.

"A mighty big apple tree to make a cupboard. And so what? It's wood like any other wood."

"Not *an* apple tree. It need not have been a cupboard either."

"What's so special about an *apple tree?*"

"*The* apple tree. Aren't you an educated boy? What does it signify?"

"I don't know, I don't care. But what about the other trees?"

"Alder," asked the old man, "and birch?" "And willow and holly," said Hugh. "And ash . . ." He waited. The old man finished it. "And oak and apple. Would you rather it had been an ordinary cupboard?" he went on.

"I don't know. Why should I tell you?"

"Then why should you expect me to answer your questions? The shop is closed. Didn't you see the notice? You are taking up my time and there is not much left of that, if you choose to destroy it as I fear you will."

"The door was open. I don't understand what you're saying."

"The sign said closed," insisted the old man. Hugh saw this sign now out of the corner of his eye, the old man edging him backwards, through the shop. Indubitably, it did say closed, in large black letters. The door was open and Hugh outside.

"I must have forgotten to lock it," the old man said and smiled and locked the door in his face and pulled down a blind, leaving Hugh foolish, baffled, and uncomfortable, alone in the cobbled street.

CHAPTER 13

HUGH took the longest way home possible: first along the river, by the crowded towpath, then around the green, through the town and past the station. He walked abstractedly, his eyes to the ground, sometimes kicking at it resentfully. The world beat outside him, but he was no part of it. When he bumped into people their glares and rebukes at once both alarmed and failed to touch him, to mean anything. He scarcely looked up or bothered to apologise, just dawdled on moodily, pushing out his lower lip, a habit he had when sulking, or rather he had used to have, for he had mostly grown out of this by now.

The crowds thinned out as Hugh left the shopping street. Walking up Chapel Road over the railway bridge, he met scarcely anyone at all.

He paused there, leaned on its painted steel wall, and rested his head upon his hands.

It was yet another separate, disconnected world he saw below. There were no trains just now, only an expanse, almost a prairie of shining steel, the criss-crossing of the parallels making a huge illusionary perspective, reaching nearly as far as he could see. It bore no relation to the railway journeys that it provided for, the familiar kind in hot and dirty trains. Yet seeing it made Hugh remember quite irrelevantly what the apple tree stood for in mythologies: immortality. King Arthur's paradise, his Avalon, had been full of apple trees – which meant . . . he thought, which meant . . .

"Hugh. *Hugh*." He almost jumped out of his skin. He had not heard the car draw up, but there it was behind him, a

96

white and rather grubby Renault. Out of it, Penn's mother leaned.

Hugh made his face as blank as it would go.

"Do you want a lift, Hugh?" she asked again. There was nothing Hugh wanted less, particularly from her just now, but his mind was beyond finding credible excuse, and his energy beyond refusing without one. For it would have needed energy to refuse her. She had a power and force which carried anyone along.

"Are you thinking of painting it?" Hugh stared at her blankly, genuinely puzzled. "You were such miles away," she said.

She was, on the face of it, the reverse of Hugh's mother, thin and dark and quick, with a brightness, a pointedness about her, and an impression, almost, of glitter. The kind of clothes she made Anna wear (always in or beyond the fashion, whatever it happened to be, or else flamboyantly scorning it) which quenched Anna, seemed to set her alight, to make her more vivid and brilliant than ever. She wore a tight black T-shirt today and white jeans, and on her head, tied gypsy-fashion, a black and white silk scarf with an actual glitter now provided by long jet earrings which swung when she moved her head.

She looked like a bird; a magpie today, she was so very black and white. Anna had said once that her mother had used to be called Hooky-Beak the Raven at school. Hugh's father who provided nicknames for most people called her Birdfeet.

His own mother, big and slow and fairish, appeared, it suddenly occurred to Hugh, a lot more likely to be the mother of the large red-headed Penn than Penn's mother did herself.

"Hop in," she said, leaning over and opening the car door

for him. But as Hugh still went on gazing at her and did not move, she patted the seat. "Get in, get in," she urged again, looking at him, her head slightly inclined, one eyebrow raised, asking questions without pronouncing them.

He armoured himself mentally against her; sat on the edge of the seat, praying for the journey to be over quickly. "You haven't shut the door properly," she said. Nor had he, Hugh found, when he tested it as if he had deliberately left himself a method of escape, however dangerous, from a moving car.

Penn's mother had always seemed far more interested in what he did, that is, his painting, than his own mother ever appeared to be, indeed far more interested than she was in the athletic achievements of her son Penn. ("What that means is having to stand for *hours, freezing,* on the edge of some muddy field; they're all so covered in mud, I can never tell which Penn *is,*" she had said once to Hugh's mother, in his hearing, though he had never heard of her actually going to watch Penn take part in any game.) But she did not show her interest in Hugh by asking questions: she was much more tactful (or subtle) than that. She broke down his guard by saying nothing or looking inquiring, amused, impressed, changing each attitude as he fathomed it for another; so that he never knew quite where he was, whether she was laughing at him or taking him seriously. He was goaded anyway into explaining or defending himself; all of which he half liked and half did not. He was relieved to be taken seriously, and he also felt that unlike most people she understood a little what he was talking about, and this made him feel less peculiar, less isolated; it even at times exhilarated him. But at other times he resented it. He did not want anyone to get inside his head, to read him with such apparent ease. Almost always when he saw her coming, he attempted to escape, and if he could not, deliberately put up his guard, resisted her interest; calling her Birdfeet in his mind, in order to shrink, belittle her. But almost always before he realised, she had broken down his guard again.

Today for once (and even in spite of the problems he felt a flicker of triumph), his preoccupations were beyond her questioning, far beyond her guessing them at all. Nor did she even try to guess, only glanced at him inquiringly as she drove him up the hill.

They were turning into their own road when Hugh was suffused by total panic. One moment it had not been there at all, the next it had taken him over completely.

"Calm *down*, Hugh," she said, as he stiffened and peered through the windscreen ahead of them. "I don't know what's the matter, what's biting you. I won't *ask*, it's not my business; just don't take it so seriously, that's all. It can't be *that* bad."

That's what you think; just for once you're wrong, thought Hugh, almost viciously, and at that moment saw the figures turn into the road, from the far end; precisely, exactly, what he feared. Yet, immediately, his fear disappeared. He felt only a distant curiosity at what the outcome of this might be. Jean, Anna and Penn in the pushchair moved inexorably up the road towards them.

They stopped abruptly. Hugh saw Anna and Jean look at each other, in horror no doubt, recognising the car in which Penn's mother drove to meet her son, now more than twelve years younger than she would have expected to find him. They must have decided that boldness was the only course, because they came on again steadily, arriving at Hugh's front gate just as the Renault drew up at the kerb beside it.

Would she recognise Penn? Hugh wondered, detachedly.

99

How could she not recognise him? Yet again how could she, without an enormous imaginative leap into the belief that such a thing was possible. In a way he wished that she would make that leap, that she would recognise Penn. For if she did – and she would have to make it for herself, nothing they said, he thought, would convince her – if she did, she would undoubtedly take charge, so relieving him of the responsibility.

"Get a move on, Hugh. Unless you want to stay in the car, that is? It's *all* the same to me."

Even so, she leaned over and opened the door for him and stayed leaning when she had let him out, looking at the baby.

"Where did you manage to steal him, Anna? Not from outside Sainsbury's, I hope?"

"Of course not," said Anna primly. "He's the brother of someone at my school." The answer must have been previously prepared, it came out so neatly, so directly. Jean, more hurried, less convincing, added:

"We said we'd look after him – so she could go out shopping."

"We've only got him for a *little* while," said Anna.

"So I should hope." But her mother spoke somewhat abstractedly, without her usual bite.

She still leaned uncomfortably across the front seat of the car, regarding intently the baby Penn who ignored her, absorbed in playing with the buckle of the pushchair belt. Even her earrings were motionless, save for the minutest flicker of light on one, which came and went without apparent cause. There was also a movement of light on the side of the car. Hugh after puzzling realised it was made by the movement of Penn's hands and the glitter of the steel buckle reflected there.

"We did think he looked a bit like those pictures of Penn

as a baby," said Anna, her face completely blank. Both Hugh and Jean jumped, Jean gasping audibly. Both stared at her. Her mother sat up abruptly. "Don't be *silly*, Anna. His hair's a bit like, that's all. I'm not sure Penn's wasn't lighter too. You are obsessed with Penn, that's your trouble. You think *everyone* looks like Penn." She pushed the seat down and fished around in the back of the car for various packages and paper bags.

"Take some of those for me, please, Hugh. Incidentally," she added, reappearing, "incidentally where *is* Penn?"

"Oh he just went off somewhere," Hugh said hurriedly, "I'm not sure where."

"You know Penn," said Anna, coolly.

"I thought I did." She was briskly gathering more parcels and handing them to Hugh, who in confusion bent to help and only succeeded in banging heads with her.

"Oh *leave* it," she said in an irritated voice. "Just shut the door for me. Have you locked it? Lock it then."

She dropped one of her paper bags while locking the door on her own side. It had Brooke Bond Tea written on it in blue letters. The two half-pound blocks of butter that fell out declared themselves to be especially imported in similar blue letters.

"Where are you taking him?" she shouted after Jean and Anna who were retreating as fast as they could up Jean's garden path. "Aren't you going to take him *home* again?"

The baby peered round the edge of the pushchair and grinned at her. Again she stared at him and again looked away.

"All babies look alike," she said to Hugh who was watching her. "Pick up that butter for me, Hugh, there's a love." But she handed him her other packages and picked it up herself before he could make a move. The bag had split, the butter almost fell out again. Each block was neatly rectangular, right-angled at one end, at the other grubby, dented, out of shape. Her fingers tried to straighten these ends to shape. Not looking, though, her eyes again were following her son, Penn.

"We're going in a minute," Anna called back.

"I just want to fetch something from indoors, that's all," said Jean.

"Be good tonight," Penn's mother said, and added as an afterthought, "Say goodnight to Penn for me, in case I don't see him. Oh and take that baby home, will you, take him home *soon*."

Hugh helped carry the things in from the car, then thankfully escaped for home. When he got back upstairs again, he went with reluctance into Jean's room, to find Anna alternately sulking and shaking with hysterical laughter, Jean curbing her, rather red in the face and cross, on the edge of tears herself, Hugh realised.

"And where have you been," she snapped at him, "leaving us to manage on our own. You didn't even say you were going out."

"I didn't know I had to."

"I suppose you haven't thought what we're going to do either?"

"No. Have you? It was all right this time anyway. She didn't recognise him."

"I almost wish she had," said Jean.

Hugh did not tell her what he had wished. But Anna stopped laughing or sulking and came out of her own world into theirs again.

"Oh no," she said, "that would have spoiled it." And hugged Penn to her, frantically. "Anyway she wouldn't have dared," she said.

Even if the infant Penn had given them much chance it would have been impossible to settle to anything that evening. Once he slept all three of them retired into separate worlds of anxiety and did not speak to one another much except by necessity. Anna sat very still wherever she found herself; Jean on the contrary never ceased to move. Hugh too roamed a great deal, from the top of the house to the bottom and back again.

All evening Hugh was afraid that his mother would question Penn's absence; was relieved that she did not, but annoyed on the other hand that she could be so vague, so careless as not to be more curious or worried as to his whereabouts. He wanted her to worry almost as much as he did not want her to.

She dropped a tray of dishes on the floor at one point. He was rent by shock. He thought at first the worst had happened, the thing he waited for and feared, before he remembered that what he feared was the discovery of Penn, which would not be heralded in such a way. From the expressions on their faces both Jean and Anna must have suffered briefly from the same fearful illusion as himself.

All three of them helped pick the dishes up again, more or less willing, but all equally irritated in reaction to the shock. Anna also looked amused. By a miracle nothing was broken except for an already cracked plate, which had split in half neatly along its crack.

"I wish you'd be more like other mothers sometimes," Jean said, her voice sharper than usual.

"Other people do occasionally drop things. Even you, Jean, I've known."

"But not all the time. You break something practically every day. Last week you broke my favourite bowl."

"Things taste the same out of other bowls."

"I think you enjoy it," said Jean bitterly, "breaking things."

"It's not what you do, *I* mind," said Hugh as bitterly, "it's what you don't do. What's funny then?" he snapped at Anna, seeing her little, separate smile.

"Nothing. *Nothing*," Anna said.

"Now leave that poor girl alone, Hugh."

"It's nothing to do with you." Hugh and his mother looked at each other, eyes half challenging, half uninterested. Her "Don't speak to me like that," came out somewhat lamely. Neither seemed to want a fight when it came to it. Hugh felt much too dreary to fight with anyone. He attacked his omelette instead. His mother finished hers quickly and absently.

"Will Penn want something when he comes in? What time *will* he be in?" she asked not with much interest, but as if she thought she ought to inquire at least. Hugh's mumble satisfied her. "I gave him my key," he added, so that she would not be surprised that the doorbell did not ring; that is, if she wondered anything.

The kitten which had slept for most of the day came to life now. It went mad, crazy, leaping huge, stiff-legged leaps from side to side, dashing from one end of the room to the other, spinning furiously in pursuit of its shadow or its tail. It seemed to turn on its own axis, it seemed weightless like a shadow, or a feather. Afterwards it tore round and round the room again, then paused, pounced, paused and pounced, time after time after time.

"All kittens behave like that," said Jean proprietorially. It helped distract them for a little while; till Hugh's father

arrived and monopolised attention as he always did. He did
not think of querying Penn's whereabouts either. He was
much more interested in Anna, plying her with plums, a
surprising number of which she ate. After a while she began
to make patterns with the stones upon her plate, taking no
notice of anyone, as if she was quite alone. Hugh tried to
attract her attention once but she ignored him.

When Hugh went to bed he tossed and turned for hours.
The landscape sucked him in eventually; he had resisted it,
clinging to his bedhead even. But the bedhead was made of
oak, which he did not know because it was painted and he
had never bothered to look any further. And the trees of
course were oak trees too, in an avenue leading towards the
castle. He had not yet reached the avenue. He was walking
along a road towards it through a grey and familiar landscape, so familiar that though he only remembered being
there four or five times, he must have visited it many other
times that he did not remember.

The sun gave no brightness. It was as if its brilliant edges
dwindled to a black centre. He stared at it fixedly for a
minute, blinding himself, and so briefly afterwards saw
nothing about him, except a kind of white, then grey haze
from which emerged gradually the grey configurations of
the landscape, defuzzing slowly, growing darker, the out-
lines clear. The broken edges of the castle were like teeth.
They offered him a threat.

Vision narrowed. It felt as if the landscape was an enormous eye, and he was at the centre of the eye. The immediate
surroundings were grey, this centre black, and it was doing
something to him that he fought against, against a force he
could not define until he realised it was trying to suck him
in; that the blackness was both the pupil of the eye and a
tunnel that was sucking, pulling him. Yet he was also still

walking along a track; towards a castle. The actions coexisted, were carried on simultaneously. At the same time he
was both screaming with fear and not screaming, feeling
the harshness of the stones beneath his feet and not feeling
them.

He struggled on. The castle grew nearer. The tunnel
sucked as hard but did not manage to pull him farther in.
The weight of the sky seemed to press on him too, pushing
him into the tunnel, into the pupil of the eye. It felt like
being drowned – only it would have to be a lake to drown
him, he thought confusedly, and not simply a tunnel. But
curiously these two forces, though together more strongly
opposing him, somehow raised in him also a still greater
obstinacy, a still greater will to resist. He was actually walking faster, and then he was running, stumbling, and the
forces were having to pursue him. He had not burst out of
them exactly, as he had burst out of the circle of alder trees
in the first dream. They were still there all round him, yet
they did not stop him going on. They were sensations as
much as forces. As he ran between the lines of oak trees – and
they were all dead he saw now – it was like a car passing
through an avenue of trees, with a little whoosh at each
tree, little stripes of sound all the way along, except that these
were stripes of feeling not of sound. Between each pair of
trees he felt the pressures grow stronger.

He passed through a vast, an enormous pressure; all the
other pressures came with him and stopped dead as he did,
and then vaporized, faded from him.

He had passed under the gate of the castle and was inside
it. He was in the courtyard, but the castle was more or less a
ruin.

He had escaped the eye, yet he was also at the centre of it
still, the eye being all around him. His footsteps were loud on

cracked cobblestones as he walked towards a studded, oaken door. The studs were multitudinous and like eyes watching him. They glinted with an iron glint that seemed out of place in this lightless, shineless world.

There was a handle on the door, shaped like a bird; a crow. As he put his hand to it the world too faded. He found himself lying in darkness, in his own bed.

Hugh woke next morning from restless sleep to the sound of infant cheerfulness next door, and water running in the bathroom. Jean was down there rinsing nappies in the basin.

"Do you know what time he woke us, Hugh? Five o'clock, five *o'clock*. And we had to keep him quiet till now. We jolly well nearly came to wake you up to help."

Upstairs in Jean's room, Anna, who had slept in the little room next door looked disapproving. "Do you know he's wet right through to the mattress."

"Well, what did you expect. Babies do, you know. It's not exactly as if we were practised at putting nappies on, and he wriggles such a lot."

Neither seemed as enthusiastic about baby-minding as they had been the day before. They were permanently on the verge of quarrelling except when united against Hugh. Anna had never sided with Jean when Penn was here, Hugh thought.

Jean said, "We'll have to say that you and Penn had breakfast early and went out, Hugh."

"Does that mean I don't get any breakfast?"

"We'll bring you something. It will probably just have to be toast or something."

"I suppose that means I'll be left to look after him," said Hugh unenthusiastically, pointing at the baby who merely grinned back inanely. "He looks positively retarded this morning."

"It's about your turn. We've had him since yesterday. Look, you can feed him too. I've managed to bring up some cereal. But for goodness sake, Hugh, keep him quiet, *whatever*."

Jean did genuinely look tired. She was as neat as usual but reminded Hugh of a cat that was not quite well, its fur a little dull and spiky. She had put on the brown-stoned brooch that her godmother had given her as a birthday present two years ago, and which she regarded as something of a charm or mascot (though she would never have admitted this), tending to wear it when she expected difficulties of some kind; from exams to a row with her father. Anna too looked tired. She was even paler than usual, chewing her tongue a lot, but neither she nor Hugh were quite so out of their depth as Jean was.

Yet all of them equally missed Penn, Hugh thought. There was a greyness over everything, as if some colours were missing from the spectrum. He felt as if they had no centre any more, were each quite separate and alone. They even moved more slowly, for the baby seemed to suck up as much of their energy as the boy Penn had given out.

Jean fortunately still remained maternal. It was she, not Anna, who checked the baby's nappy before she went downstairs, that it was not wet, or falling off him, and she who set out Penn's food, and who looked round the room to see that they had left nothing dangerous. Anna merely stood and watched. Nor did she kiss the baby when Jean did, rather awkwardly. But if she was less concerned about Penn as a baby, she was more concerned about him as Penn, turning as they went out of the room and, for a longish moment, gazing at him.

Hugh and Penn were left to regard each other, to stare each other out; this almost their first proper confrontation, for Hugh had carefully avoided one till now. Uncomfortable, he was the first to look away. "Da," said the infant Penn, and held out the sodden and unattractive-looking cloth which up till then he had been stuffing in his mouth. When Hugh did not immediately respond, the baby suddenly realised that he did not know him, that both the more familiar girls had gone. He started to crawl frantically towards the door. His mouth squared up and let out an enormous howl.

Hugh, as frantically, grabbed him back. He tried tickling Penn, bumped him up and down, made every face he could think of. The baby stopped wailing after a moment, but stared at him unblinking, unamused. He felt as foolish as an unsuccessful comic, was about to set him on the floor again when Penn jabbed a finger painfully right into his eye. It was Hugh who felt like howling now.

"Blast you, Penn," he said, and saying the name, had a sudden desperate vision: that this was Penn, his friend. He could not bear to think of that Penn now. Firmly he shut him from his mind and remembered breakfast with relief; Weetabix and milk in a rabbit-covered bowl. Before Penn could start to wail again he thrust out a spoonful of the Weetabix – Penn obligingly opening his mouth, but shutting it again as the spoon arrived, so that it merely collided with his face and the Weetabix was scattered, mostly on the floor. The next time, also, Penn opened his mouth to the approaching spoon only to push it aside with a hand and blow, simultaneously, again effectively dispersing cereal, now largely over Hugh. Hugh fetched a towel, spread it on the floor and sat the baby in the middle of it. "You can jolly well feed yourself then," he said grimly and handed Penn the bowl and spoon. The next five minutes' peace was, he decided, worth the mess, eating Weetabix with fingers not being exactly a tidy or a clean pursuit.

And after breakfast when Penn had first emptied out Jean's waste-paper basket and devoured a rotten apple-core, then attempted to annihilate Jean's collection of glass animals (not that that would have been much loss, Hugh thought privately) noisily resisting all attempts meanwhile to interest him in the toys provided, Hugh reverted to the only proper distraction that he knew of: paint. There were two old tins of powder colour among his other materials. He mixed them, found sheets of newspaper and his oldest brushes, dabbing the newspaper with paint to encourage the baby and demonstrate the possibilities. The baby was much more interested in decorating itself than the paper, and by hand rather than by brush, but it freed Hugh for another five minutes, more or less, until Anna and Jean arrived back from breakfast with some leathery slices of toast for him.

Jean gasped, seeing the room.

"You didn't have to let him make such an awful mess. It's *awful*, Hugh."

"You must be joking," Hugh said wearily. "If I ever have babies, I'm going to keep them in cages till they're old enough to be civilised. He practically gouged my eye out. Look."

"Just look at his cereal. It's everywhere. And paint, Hugh, paint for a baby of his age. You must be out of your mind."

"I suppose you would rather that he'd howled the place down," said Hugh and saw Anna smile secretly, "or broken all your glass animals. They're hideous anyway."

"Hugh, you've got to do something. We can't go on like this." Jean was scarlet in the face.

"Something like what?"

"Like . . . don't be so negative, Hugh."

"Well, have you any ideas then?"

"I can't," she wailed, "I can't."

"Well, nor have I. Unless we all get in the cupboard ourselves. That'll be the end of it. We'll be babies too, no one will be able to make us do anything."

"No," said Jean. "*No*." Hugh could feel her terror, that she could scarcely speak for it, letting it run away with her.

"We could go and see that old man of yours," Anna said quietly to Hugh.

"What old man?" He feigned incomprehension. "Oh *him*. Just what good do you think he'd do?" He thought to himself, that's truer than you know; for nothing at all had come out of his going yesterday. The old man had been very unhelpful and was just as likely to be unhelpful today, the situation being still the same. Positively he did not want to go back to him again. He was sick of the whole business suddenly. He wanted to go away, to shut everything out and paint. ALONE, he thought; BY MYSELF. The thought was as loud to him as a spoken voice. It commanded him; so that he even turned to go out of the room, all the reasons why he should stay wiped clean out of his mind. He felt quite slippery, like a fish, slipping in and out of things, engaging nowhere, touching nothing.

"Where are you going? You *can't* go away," Jean shouted after him.

"All right, let's put him in the cupboard again," Hugh said pointing at Penn, who was sitting in the centre of the room regarding them. The thought only came to his mind as he spoke.

"Are you serious?"

"Of course I am" (which was mostly, though, a lie).

"It *is* an idea," said Anna thoughtfully. Hugh looked at her with almost as much surprise as Jean did.

"But I don't see . . ."

"We've never tried putting anything back in there, have we? Something we've already changed." Nor had they; which struck Hugh now as odd, almost odd enough not to be an accident. "Suppose it worked the other way," went on Anna, persuasively.

"Just supposing it *didn't?*" Jean asked. She sounded calmer now. Even so her interruptions were irrelevant, more or less, Hugh and Anna discussing this as just between themselves.

"He'd only be younger . . ." said Hugh. "We wouldn't be worse off, would we?"

"It might be better," Anna said.

"It's all crazy, it couldn't be worse," Jean pushed her voice in forcibly.

"We could experiment with something else first, couldn't we," said Anna.

The infant Penn had started to crawl towards the door. They all suddenly saw and stopped and watched him.

"He *wants* to go himself," said Anna, drawing in her breath. They watched him pull the door open and disappear round it. They heard the door of Hugh's room pulled open in its turn – at which they all three looked at one another and followed. "Well, at least we won't need to clean him up," said Hugh. Penn went straight for the cupboard. Jean gasped and ran to pull him out, but it was the tidier, the more obvious course, to let go, to shut the door on him. Hugh automatically, without any conscious decision-taking, removed Jean, and Anna, gently, carefully this time, closed the cupboard door. It felt as if another inevitable piece had been fitted into a pattern in which they and everything they knew now formed a part. Then – it was half-past nine on an

August Friday – they opened the door again, to find what looked like an almost new-born baby lying there blinking up at them.

Their first thought was uniform, even Jean's; not shock or fear or horror. Hugh, without looking at them, knew neither of the others felt any of those, any more than he did himself. What he felt – and they felt – was a huge and quite simple awe.

The baby was so tiny, so puny and shrivelled. It could not have been more than a few days' old. But its face looked as old as an old man's face, the skin all dried and wrinkled round its eyes and ears. Its legs kicked thin as a sparrow's legs from the fat white folds of its napkin. When Jean laid it gently down on Hugh's bed it lay with its eyes wide open, dark yet milky, staring up at the ceiling, and there was a piece of fluff in the centre of one eye, like a flaw in glass. How odd it was, Hugh thought, that the baby did not seem to mind the fluff. He watched its mouth opening and shutting, its arms and legs moving randomly, slowly. It was there in the room with the rest of them and yet somehow far away, kicking and hitting at something none of them could see.

CHAPTER 14

JEAN and Anna took turns at carrying the baby down the hill. Penn was much too small to go in the pushchair now, and there was no possibility of getting hold of a pram instead. They had found a shawl in the tallboy from which both the button box and the napkins had come – it must have been white once, but was now faintly yellow and smelt of mothballs, this for Hugh adding to the feeling of unreality. It reminded him of occasions quite other than these, little flashes of himself as a child playing with something or dreaming or watching his mother turn out those same drawers, digging in them frenetically like a terrier in order to find some garment or piece of material.

The baby, well-wrapped in first the shawl and then a check tablecloth to disguise its existence as far as possible, was asleep; well-fed, replete. Despite the circumstances both Jean and Anna looked faintly pleased with themselves, as well they might, thought Hugh, having observed with surprise the somewhat technical operations necessary for feeding it.

The baby had begun whimpering not long after it came out of the cupboard. "It must be hungry," Jean and Anna had said more or less simultaneously, and both had turned and looked at Hugh.

"Why are you looking at me? I don't know the first thing about feeding babies." Hugh felt that this was one problem he could quite legitimately shunt off on to their shoulders.

But neither Anna nor Jean, it appeared, knew much about feeding babies either. They seemed scared by Penn's smallness, holding him gingerly as if he was about to break. They could have given Penn a bottle, but did not know how to prepare it, and had to scour the house for discarded baby manuals which would instruct them. Everything had to be sterilised by boiling, it appeared, including the water to make up the feed, and there had to be the right proportion of milk and the right proportion of water, and to assess that they had to know the baby's weight. All of this meant expeditions to the kitchen, first to weigh Penn on Hugh's mother's old-fashioned scales – half the brass weights were missing which did not help – then to boil pans of water, Hugh keeping guard meanwhile in case his mother came. The baby continued wailing on and off, a small noise like a kitten, but very persistent, It made little sucking, snuffling sounds, trying unavailingly to eat its thumb as a substitute for food.

For distraction, to protect himself from this, Hugh read out extracts from the baby manual when anyone was around to hear.

"The one thing a mother needs to know; what is best for baby's needs and what sort of balance is best to aim at, breast or bottle. Let mother choose herself, and what suits her is bound to be good for baby," he read. This only had the effect of annoying further the already agitated Jean and Anna who dispatched him therefore to buy a tin of milk from the supermarket, and a teat from the chemist, a task he disliked still more because it would mean facing the same assistant again as yesterday. He did not, fortunately, have to buy a bottle, as Jean had found one at the back of the airing-cupboard.

There was a queue in the chemist's this time, though still only one assistant. As he waited he heard a familiar voice behind him.

"Hugh," it said, and he turned round, startled, to find the

person of all that he least wanted to see: Penn's mother
again. Her dark eyes this morning were ringed with black –
whether from paint or exhaustion he could not tell – but she
reminded him less of a bird than one of the small nocturnal
mammals in the zoo; in particular a bushbaby. It seemed
extraordinary that he had been looking at bushbabies only
two days ago. It felt more like a hundred years.

The colour had run into his face. He could feel it and was
so annoyed that he attempted to make himself as nonchalant
as Anna yesterday.

"Did you have a good evening? Did you get in very late?"
he asked, before she could say any more, and was doing
quite well listening to her (if without hearing much), even
managing to interpolate the odd and he hoped relevant
comment, when he noticed that the queue ahead of him had
dwindled, and the last person in it, an old woman in a fat
green hat, was handing over the money for a box of corn-
plasters, two tubes of toothpaste, and a tin of blackcurrant
throat pastilles.

Immediately the horror of the situation came back to him.
He could not ask for the teat in front of Penn's mother. Even
if she was unlikely to connect it with Penn, she would be
bound to be curious as to why he wanted it, or anyway
would look amused, which might in its way be as tiresome.
In either case she was quite likely to mention it to Hugh's
mother, making a joke of it, and then Hugh's mother would
want to know why too.

Mumbling something he shot across the shop to a display
of extravagantly wrapped and ribboned soaps at which he
stood, with all the appearance of total absorption, but
actually seeing none of them.

"You'll pay half as much again for the wrapping if you
buy those," said the voice of Penn's mother. "If you want

soap wrapped, why don't you buy it separately and wrap it up yourself; a creative gent like you."

Hugh stared fixedly at three pale green heart-shaped cakes in a heart-shaped green box, labelled Amour – Springtime.

"Can I *help* you," came another voice, for the third time of asking, he realised; only he had not taken it in before, or that it was addressed to him.

"Help her first," he said somewhat desperately, pointing at Penn's mother. "I'm not in any hurry."

"No, no, Hugh. I'm not in a hurry either. Get what you want first." This might even have been intentionally malicious, he thought.

"Take your time then," said the assistant, pert as ever, in a pink overall today, which was all Hugh saw of her. He snatched from the rack before him the cheapest and smallest-looking soap he saw, shaped like a lemon, and wrapped in tissue paper.

"That's eightpence to you," she said coolly, and he paid it reluctantly, hoping he'd still have enough left for the things he had to buy and thinking that Anna and Jean must be cursing him by now for taking such a time.

"Hope they took that baby back," Penn's mother threw at him then, making his stomach turn. But she was asking for Elastoplast as he gathered up his soap, so he was able to escape with no more than a smile directed vaguely at her back. He went next door purposefully, to the newsagent's, and stood gazing at boxes of felt-tipped pens and sinister floppy rubber insects. He had been afraid that Penn's mother might follow him there too, but to his relief saw her leave the chemist's, climb into her car, the white Renault standing by the pavement, and drive off smartly with the minimum of preparatory fumbling; as neat and direct a performance as any of Penn's on some sports field. She waved as she went.

Hugh was not sure whether this was meant for him or some other acquaintance she had caught sight of.

He went determinedly back to the chemist's shop, not letting apprehension near him. To his relief it was empty now, except for the assistant in her pink nylon overall.

"Large, medium or small?" she asked standing on a stool to get the teat from a shelf above the counter.

"Large . . . *what?*" asked Hugh baffled, gazing firmly at her ankles. "Hole, of course; in the teat. Large, medium or small. Wake up, dozey, make up your mind," she urged as Hugh hesitated. "I can't stand up here all day, anyone would think you liked looking at my legs." And she giggled again.

"Small, I suppose." Hugh plunged for it, thinking of the smallness of the baby.

"Got an addition to the family?" she asked as she put the teat in a paper bag. "Not exactly." Hugh had been about to add something lame about it being for a friend's baby, then decided that it was nothing to do with her. Why shouldn't he buy a teat if he wanted to, why should he be obliged to explain? So he handed over his money and emerged from the shop almost dizzy with relief at having obtained it safely, so dizzy indeed that he forgot the tin of milk and had to turn back to the supermarket where he waited behind a woman buying a dozen tins of pilchards, for her children, it appeared, not cats. (If it had been for her cats, she explained to Hugh, she would have bought the kind without tomato sauce.)

Between them afterwards they had only a halfpence left. We'll make Penn contribute, Hugh thought. After all, the money had been spent on him. Meanwhile, he did not know what they would do if they needed to buy anything else.

They fed the baby in Penn's own room, which was the one

corresponding to Hugh's in the next-door house. It seemed
safer there. Anna did not think her mother would come
back now till the afternoon, whereas in Hugh and Jean's
house, their mother might in theory appear at any
minute.

The small-holed teat turned out wrong, naturally. It
appeared that the smaller the baby, the larger the necessary
hole, because small babies sucked so much less powerfully.
"But how was I supposed to know that?" asked Hugh with
disgust, as the baby sucked valiantly, but with little success
until it occurred to him to enlarge the hole with a needle
made red-hot in a match flame. After that the feed pro-
ceeded more easily.

They took it in turns to give the bottle. Hugh had watched
first Anna then Jean feed the baby for a little while, each
holding it more easily as they grew used to it, sitting very
still, smiling a little, gazing most intently at its face. A
sudden and quite unexpected longing had come over Hugh
to feed the baby too, and when he thought Anna had had
long enough, he removed it from her firmly, sat down on
Penn's bed, baby somewhat awkwardly in one hand, bottle
in the other.

Its nails looked papery but were surprisingly long and
sharp. The clutch of its small and curly fingers, the small pull
of its suck against the bottle, made him feel strange; with the
same awe that he had felt first seeing the baby, but added to
that now a curious softness, a curious warmth. He felt he
must look as intent and rapt as Jean and Anna had. Neither of
them objected to his feeding the baby. Indeed neither even
seemed surprised, though Jean was inclined to tease a little,
fiddling as she watched him with her brown-stoned brooch.
Anna did not take her eyes off either of them, Hugh or the
baby.

As Hugh sat with the small warmth of the baby against him, his eyes began to wander round the room at the evidence of Penn's mostly sporting activities; a cricket bat, two tennis rackets, a squash racket, all arranged in meticulous order, for Penn was – had been – meticulously neat. There were books on sport on a shelf, others by a man called Masefield, two by Conrad, and one called *The Cruel Sea*. Next to them was a silver cup won for school athletics, and pinned under the shelf above the bed, a row of photographs of sportsmen mostly, footballers and cricketers, but one of Jane Fonda, dressed in leather fringes; all the paraphernalia of Penn's ordinary life, as Hugh had always known it.

It made Hugh suddenly miss wretchedly the real Penn. It made him ache. That these minute fingers now clutching him could ever hold the bat or the rackets was nearly inconceivable. Compared to the baby they looked grotesquely huge. He thought of Gulliver in Brobdingnag, for looked at from the baby's size, the graining of willow on the cricket bat, of oak on the bookshelves, looked crude and coarse and the gut strings of the racket, swollen, positively disgusting; even the books and the silver cup might have been for giants to read and to display.

Hugh shook himself roughly and made his eyes see from his own proper adolescent size and not from the minuteness of the baby's. At that moment Anna removed Penn from him firmly. "It's my turn again now," she said. "You've had him ages."

Hugh did not take another turn. The level of milk went down so slowly, he thought, hoped, they might be here for the rest of the morning. But at half-past eleven Jean said with a gasp, "Look at the time. We'll have to hurry, or we won't have time before lunch." They decided, she and Anna, to abandon the last ounce. The baby was almost asleep now and kept on forgetting to suck, except once, twice, lazily, when prodded hard.

It was not Hugh's idea that they should go back to the junk shop and certainly not his wish. But he had to admit that there was absolutely nothing else they could do. Nor could he explain his reluctance, because he was unwilling to reveal his visit yesterday, for reasons he could not define, beyond the fact that it had been a waste of effort. This added to his pessimism now.

While organising the feed, the sheer pressure of activity had driven away their fear, had stopped them wondering what could happen next. But they were on the edge of things – just as activity buoyed them up, elated them, as easily they were plunged back into apprehension, into fear. They plunged now. Going down the hill no one spoke at all. Vehicles loomed at them from the road; cars, vans, lorries had never seemed noisier, more startling. Every person they met might have been about to discover the baby, take it away from them.

Hugh saw trees. He might never have seen trees before, because it dawned on him suddenly for the first time that they were no more than giant plants. Looked at as trees they were normal, unexceptional, but looked at as giant plants, they became grotesque; they became threatening, even the smallest of them. In their prosperous suburb, there were trees everywhere. Whichever way he looked, he saw them; giant plants; enemies.

The shop was shut and looked empty. The windows were so dusty it was hard to see anything beyond, even on the window shelf. By pressing his face to the glass and screwing up his eyes Hugh could make out a few dim shapes, but that was all. The screen of dust might have been formed deliberately to hide them from the outside world. Other people must have come to the conclusion that the shop was empty too, because two posters with flowing lettering to advertise a pop group called Stoned Crow had been posted in one corner of the window. CLOSED, said the notice on the door.

Having got so far in spite of his reluctance to come, Hugh did not intend to go away without seeing the old man. He took the door handle and rattled it furiously, at the same time knocking at the glass with his other hand. Jean and Anna stood a few paces behind him, Anna holding the baby.

"But if he's *shut*," Jean was saying despairingly.

On the other side of the door, within the shop, Hugh thought he discerned faint movements. Rage overcame him, he was determined to get an answer, rattling and knocking harder than ever. "You'll break the door down," Jean said anxiously. But the door had suddenly removed itself from his hands and stood wide open.

The old man blinked in the daylight, his voice came slight and querulous. "What do you want? Can't you see I'm closed."

Hugh said fiercely, "You've got to let us in."

"Got to. *Got* to. I don't understand that."

"You know perfectly well who I am. You must help us, you must." The old man looked at him with what appeared to be dislike. "Must, *must*. Must, is it?" He stared at each of them in turn. Hugh and Anna both stared back unblinkingly, but Jean, uneasily, turned away her head. He did not look at the baby in Anna's arms, just touched it briefly with an expression across his face that Hugh could not read. The baby stirred but did not wake.

"Come in. If you *must*," the old man said at last.

"We must," Hugh said, and stepped across the threshold. The two girls followed him.

"You chose the cupboard yourself. You did not buy it because I persuaded you."

Hugh did not reply. He was looking round the shop. As he had guessed when peering from outside it was even emptier than yesterday. There were still the objects – all with that same face – but fewer; there was still the same sense of recognition, yet if anything he could trace it even less than yesterday. The old man had disappeared again, and they stood in the middle of the shop waiting for his return. Hugh found himself overcome with unexpected embarrassment, wishing himself anywhere else but here. He shrank from the thought of having to explain himself again, of having to ask questions. He wished he could shut his eyes and vanish. He did not mind how or where.

The old man returned to the shop very differently. He was almost jovial. "Now what can I do to help?" he asked as if they were favoured customers. They stared at him in surprise, but no one said anything. Jean looked anxiously at Hugh, but Hugh ignored the message. Anna had begun wandering round the shop, picking things up and putting them down again; peering at pictures on the walls; wiping off dust with her fingers where she wanted to examine more closely. She had given the baby to Jean to hold.

"Now then, you must have come for something. You'd better tell me quickly or I shall have to send you away again." But he said it as if he was joking.

"You know," said Hugh, "you know perfectly well. The cupboard," he added reluctantly, the old man looking at him, still with a smile but without a word. "You've got to help. Look, that's Penn, that baby. He should be the same age as me. But look what it's done to him."

"What did you expect? I don't see why you're complaining. It's a fine child."

"I told you." Hugh, goaded, was getting angrier. "Just a cupboard to put my clothes in. And just look now." He pointed at Penn.

"Well, and what ideas have you?"

"None," admitted Hugh.

"He did have one. He said we should all get into the cupboard ourselves. But what good would that do?" asked Jean, rather loud and shrill at first, reducing the volume halfway through because of the baby sleeping in her arms.

The old man spoke to Hugh. "You have already been inside it."

Hugh stared at him. "What do you mean?"

"Use your brain," said the old man mildly.

"I wanted to be inside it. I nearly got into it. But I didn't. Otherwise what happened to Penn would have happened to me."

"What happened to Penn frightened you a good deal more than it frightened him."

"He's just a baby now. He wouldn't understand anything."

"*You* were frightened."

"I don't know." Hugh spoke with less certainty. But as he spoke a coldness came over him; at first a wave of cold, and then a swifter one of heat – panic – which swept through every part of him from his fingers to his feet; like a river with many tributaries. He shook with fear. He had to sit down, but there was nothing to sit on except a chest with a curious cane top, from which, almost immediately, he rose, realising its fragility, only to reseat himself with infinite care. It was illogical, he knew, to rise and sit again – if the cane had not broken the first time when he had sat so abruptly, it was unlikely to break the second, gentler time; equally this would not remedy damage already done. But it was as if he had to prove his recognition of the need for care and to establish that he had not been totally swept away by terror. It was all quite useless anyway, he thought; the fear filtered through him more gently, slowly; gradually ebbed, receded, from consciousness.

"I was scared out of my mind." He admitted it.

"You have the fear and he does not, you've got to decide and he has not."

"You've said all that before. It doesn't help."

"The cupboard is more powerful than you think. In a sense it has drawn you in already. You have already been inside it."

"What do you mean? I *haven't*."

"I don't understand either," said Jean as if she was defending Hugh. The old man turned from her, more towards Hugh.

"You've only got to use your brains, boy."

"Do you mean those dreams?"

"Dreams, dreams, if you have to call them that. If you only accept the categories you know already." The old man sounded infinitely scornful.

"There's nothing wrong with dreams."

"Who said there was. Don't be so touchy, boy."

"*Me* touchy." But in fact Hugh was more engrossed by the problem now.

He said slowly, "It was some other sort of world. Like Thomas the Rhymer's – something like that. But it wasn't any more real than dreams; or any less, come to that."

"Who said it was?"

"It was real in its way, its own way." As Hugh spoke he noticed Jean staring at him, her face wide-open with astonishment; she looked ridiculous, he thought. "What isn't?" asked the old man. "What isn't real in its own way?" And then, "What was wrong with being frightened?"

Hugh said crossly, "You keep changing the subject. You keep on asking me the same questions and not answering any. We keep on going round and round in circles."

"Was it so bad?" insisted the old man.

"I wasn't frightened then."

"But you were just now?"

"That was just for Penn," Hugh said.

"Because he did not come out?"

"If I went in, I came out the same. How could I if he didn't? Anyway what happened to me is beside the point. It's *him*, Penn, we're here about."

"All right, you were frightened. But is that important? If so, I suppose, naturally, you want to do something."

"You talk as if this was an ordinary thing to happen. It's reasonable enough to want some way out – of a thing like this—" Hugh indicated Penn again. "Of *course* I want an answer."

"You could call it an answer. The name is unimportant."

"In which case I'll call what happened to me dreams. Why can't you talk sense?" said Hugh, furiously.

("What's in a name," Anna quoted dreamily in what he would have called a very prissy voice, the first time she had spoken since they left the house.) Hugh was angry in part because totally confused. It was like a conversation in a dream in which no comment related or led on to any other.

"We want Penn back at his own proper age," he said speaking loudly and clearly, as if to an idiot or a foreigner. "I'm asking you for advice not for philosophy." He was offensive intentionally.

"But you already know. You don't need advice. You're only resisting it. You have been into that other world. Now go into it again, but deliberately. And go on into your castle."

Hugh drew in his breath. "There really is a castle?" he asked slowly.

"Don't you believe it yet?"

"I didn't mean it quite like that."

On a table nearby there was a chessboard set out. The kings, both black and white, had faces, the same face of course as all the others. And there were the castles – the obviousness of this annoyed Hugh as his gaze fell on them. Yet still he could not stop himself reaching out and picking up one black and one white castle, one in either hand, balancing, turning them, setting them down again. The black castle was slightly the heavier of the two. An ebony castle, he thought, and an ivory castle; a castle of wood and another of bone. "Corny," he said aloud, still irritated. "Corny. I bet you put them out on purpose. They weren't here yesterday."

The old man picked up the white castle now and stroked and held it, cupped between his hands. "In the castle you can try to decide. You will see what the choices are, as they are, not as you see them now."

Hugh was observing the way the castle trembled in his hands. They were knotted, with huge blue veins, very old, very shrivelled hands. He was such an *old* man, he realised, and felt an inconvenient, disconcerting sympathy and pity; which made him feel guilty at his own impatience. Age made you ramble as the old man had seemed to ramble. And yet always within his words there had been this uncompromising edge.

The sleeping baby in Jean's arms pursed up its lips with its usual sucking sound. Hugh looked from him to the old man and back again, drawing in his breath at the likeness between them; the way both appeared withered, flesh narrow over bone. Almost for the first time he could see a progression between birth and youth and age; not as unlinked stages –

like snapshots, or separate beads on a string – baby, child, youth, young man, middle-aged then old man – but as one steady progression from each stage to the next. That would be his own progression. He had never related it to himself before, or only vaguely, not with this total, piercing comprehension.

"Do I wait for it – till I dream again?" he asked more gently, because of this inconvenient pity he had felt.

"It is *not* a dream."

"Yes but it's a word – and convenient."

"Go into the cupboard. Don't wait till it pulls you. Go into it freely. *Then* you will have power."

"By myself?" Hugh asked.

"Don't be stupider than necessary; all four of you."

"I don't have to go?" Jean looked more terrified than ever. "I couldn't go."

"Especially you."

"Oh *please*," Jean said. "Oh *please*, oh *please*."

"Don't worry. It won't hurt you. It has no power over you."

"Must *I* go?" asked Anna.

"What do you think?" said the old man.

"Is it dangerous for any of us?" asked Hugh.

"You wear me out with questions. I'm an old man," he answered querulously, almost whining. When asked outright for pity, Hugh stopped feeling it. "You'd better tell us, you must," he said growing angry again.

"*Must?* Of course it's dangerous. Use your wits. It could be destructive."

"Of what?" asked Hugh.

"Of what you decide. You must destroy something."

"We only want Penn back at his proper age, that's all we want." Jean was crying now, tears pouring down her cheeks.

She had to give the baby to Anna to hold so that she could hunt for a handkerchief.

"Do you? How easy you make it sound. The damage will not be to you, however, or anything you could see. You are blind and fortunate."

"Is that all you have to say?" asked Hugh.

"Isn't it enough?" The old man spoke more querulously than ever. His voice sounded very tired. There was a silence in which all three of them looked at one another and looked away uncertainly, and from which, suddenly, the old man, having seemingly forgotten their existence, swung round on Anna and spoke in a flood of words, his voice now stronger than it had been all morning. They listened to him, puzzled and amazed.

"Of course I look ordinary. What do you expect? All of us were ordinary in most respects. To be remarkable for so many thousand years would be intolerable. Everything is ordinary – dying, loving, being born – it's dirty sheets and bowls of water, and what to get for breakfast and what for supper, and eating breakfast and eating supper. It always was, it always is; except sometimes, occasionally, the looking and hearing and feeling. And there's not much time for that now, you are wasting all my time."

They watched him, mute, almost holding in the sound of breath. The old man's voice had wandered towards the end. Now it hardened again.

"Go away, all of you. You've asked enough questions and you've worn me out. I need what strength I have and I need what time. Go away. Please *go away*."

Hugh looked back as they went out. For a brief moment before the door was slammed on them and the bolts noisily drawn, he saw the old man's face, very pale and as if hanging in mid-air, his body vanished in the dimness and beyond him all the other faces, carved or painted or engraved, from the chess kings of ebony and ivory to the brown-spotted prints on the walls. The blind white head was in a corner. He had not noticed it this morning, not till now, but it too he realised bore the same features as the others.

"What was it all about? That last thing?" he asked Anna as they started up the hill. They had dropped behind Jean (who was no longer crying, but walked silently and with an unusual rigidity) and spoke only to each other. Hugh needed to talk, but was concerned not to let Jean be more terrified than she was already. "He seemed to be talking to you, Anna," he said, "particularly."

"Didn't you see all those faces?" Anna asked. Hugh knew what she was going to say next; had known it all the time, but not quite wanted to know.

"They were all the same face. They were all of him only younger, some younger than others."

"In the prime of life," Hugh said. He tested Anna. "But they all came from different periods. There was a Roman head and an eighteenth-century print and a mediaeval . . ."

"He had the cupboard," Anna said, "or whatever it was. Perhaps it wasn't a cupboard always."

"But then why . . .?" pressed Hugh. Anna interrupted him. "I was thinking how ordinary he looked if it worked like that, if he has been alive so long. He must have heard my thought," she said. She smiled at Hugh tentatively. Hugh, lightly, touched her on the arm. And a moment later, touched her arm again.

He said no more. He was working out for himself what the old man had said from the confusion of words and phrases that were moving in his head. For the conversation had progressed sideways, at angles, never reaching or concluding anything.

The decision lay in his power; he could rescue Penn. But first he had to go into the cupboard of his own accord. That would take him into the other world again, and then he would enter the castle. He had only been into it by chance before, because the power of the cupboard had drawn him in. It had controlled his coming and controlled his going. But if he went into it by his own will, then the magic could neither hold nor release him except as he chose. The magic would in part belong to him for that little while; he might control it.

But he could not control his perceptions now. Coming down the hill all trees had startled him. Going up he saw only the apple trees. They jumped out at him from every garden. He seemed to see nothing else.

CHAPTER 15

HUGH's mother called out from the kitchen as they went quietly up the stairs. "Hugh, Jean, food's nearly ready." "Five minutes, *five*," Hugh shouted back.

They shut the door of his room and wedged it with a chair. As usual they had to wait for Anna who insisted on combing her hair as carefully as if she was preparing for a school speech-day. But at last, still without saying anything, they climbed into the cupboard, first Anna, holding the baby – she had taken it from Jean without a word, just holding out her arms, Jean surrendering without protest – then Jean, then last, Hugh himself. He had intended to leave the door open, but involuntarily gave a tug on the tie-rail and the door clicked into place behind him. "Don't shut the other one, *don't*," Jean pleaded. Hugh had had no intention of it, yet the door swung shut, seemingly of its own accord, set off by the movement of the other one. He put out his hand to stop it too late, for the latch caught, and when he tried pushing it open, it appeared to have jammed. He could not open either door.

Jean was sobbing quietly beneath her breath. She was trying to disguise it, but every now and then a louder one broke out as a hiccup and a gasp. Hugh felt for her hand in the darkness and took it and squeezed it, and she squeezed back gratefully. He wanted to take Anna's hand too, tentatively put out his own, but as he hesitated heard a whimper and remembered that she was holding the baby.

The baby whimpered again. The whole cupboard smelt of baby, the faintly sweet animal smell of milk, wet nappy

132

and talcum powder. It was a big cupboard – yet Hugh
would have expected it to feel much more crowded than it
did with the three of them and Penn inside it. But it felt as
if the darkness reached for miles behind him, as if the back of
the cupboard was not there at all, and when he reached out
his spare hand it was almost a shock to find the cool grain of
the wood beneath his fingers.

The grain, the whole feel of the wood was good, comfort-
ing. Hugh traced it out, his fingers almost as seeing as eyes,
and he took Jean's hand, the one he held, and placed it on the
wood, so that she could feel it and be comforted as well.

He did not remember ever holding Jean's hand before. As
a family they did not often hug or kiss or touch. Penn and
Anna's family was much more demonstrative.

There was a sound in the cupboard now, a single note, yet
containing all notes. At first it emerged from a single point,
but then it hissed and swelled, spread further as if beyond the
walls, as if thrown out into an enormous void. But at the
same time it seemed to have joined itself into a narrower line
of sound, like a telegraph wire above Hugh's head, and he
reached up his hand to find the brass hanging-rail which felt
as thin and hard as he expected, but also alive, as if full of
electricity, making his wrists, his arms, his hands tingle and
shake with sound, with the echoings it threw so far away.
The echoes seemed held and thrown by other places too.
Hugh felt them by his hips but thinner, from the tie-rail that
must have been, also by his head in triplicate, a more florid,
curling sound, no doubt emerging from the three brass
hooks. The sound ran down his arms, up into his head, until
it seemed filled with the same echoes, filled with humming,
heated wires, hissing, swelling, exploding. It was unbearable.
Hugh cried out sharply, dropped Jean's hand and clutched at
his head with both hands. The echoes died. The darkness

faded. It was like being in some vehicle, rushing towards a group of trees, the vision glassy and shimmering with the speed of it. He put out his hands to protect his head from collision, but then the world steadied about him. He was standing on the edge of a wood, dizzy still, but no longer moving, quiet, in one place.

"That was a real bramble, it really hurt," said an indignant voice. He looked round to see Jean holding out her leg, with a line of red beads in one place on a white graze.

"And that's real blood, so it can't be a dream, Hugh."

"Who said it was a dream?" Jean looked at him and nodded. She seemed much calmer. She was no longer crying, nor looked as if she wanted to. They stood side by side looking about them. The wood at their backs was low and scrubby, with untidy undergrowth, brambles and nettles and stunted saplings, and underfoot dead twigs and branches and the bleached-out leaves of many autumns; soft beneath but still faintly crisp on top.

"Look, apples," Jean said, and Hugh's eyes following hers saw a young apple tree. It had only four apples on it, much too round and weighty for the slender tree. "They're ripe," Jean said, "do you think we dare eat one?" Hugh was tempted too. As Jean was not tall enough, he himself reached up and picked the nearest green though ripe-looking apple, but an instinctive caution stopped him taking a bite out of it. "I'm not sure. I'm not sure it would be safe. Perhaps we'd better not." Jean, cautious herself, accepted his caution without argument. Hugh put the apple in the pocket of his jeans where it made an awkward bulge and rubbed against his thigh as he moved. It was the first time in this place he had not been wearing pyjamas, he realised. How absurd he must have looked here in striped pyjamas from Marks and Spencers. Though this thought had never occurred to him at the time of wearing them, yet he did undoubtedly feel easier in his jeans and T-shirt. He felt more in control of what he did. He felt part of the country, belonging to it, instead of standing out as an intruder, a stranger, even though on the face of it jeans and T-shirts were no more appropriate.

The familiar landscape reached away. Part of its very familiarity, he thought, lay precisely in the way it changed each time he came, not just seasonally but in its very features. What was absent to his eyes was still held in his mind, was part of what he saw – just as some aspects of a friend may not be visible yet still remain part of him. And that, he knew, was a good analogy; this landscape assuming personality, assuming life as landscape in his own familiar world did not. There was no lake today for instance, but he recognised other landmarks – folds and dips and rises, groups and avenues of trees. The castle dominated everything. It was whole, no longer ruined, no longer forbidding, wrapped in sunlight, slumbering, peaceful. Yet it was also the centre of a vortex, drawing everything in towards it on invisible threads. It was like the twist of a kaleidoscope. The same elements formed a different pattern, but the pattern had always been present in the elements. The castle assumed only its obvious, rightful place.

"Is that where we're going? Is that your castle?"

"I guess so; I can't see another one."

"You've been here before. How many times?"

"Every night since the cupboard came. That I remember anyway." Jean drew in her breath. "Have you been into the castle?" "Only once, that I remember. And not right inside, just into a courtyard. It was ruined then." Hugh wished he had not added this. Jean's voice became higher, more anxious. "But how could it be? It isn't ruined now."

"It was probably just the way I saw it," he said to comfort her and wondered, fleetingly, if this could be true, the ruins coming in truth from his own mind.

Jean said wonderingly, "I didn't know it would be like *this*."

"Like how?"

"Ordinary."

"*Ordinary?*" asked Hugh.

"Grass and trees and brambles which prick you. It's like the park. I mean, like any walk." "What did you think it would be like?" "I don't know, I didn't think – I couldn't – but not like this. Like any bit of country. And it's such a fantastic day."

It was, too, the best day of any that Hugh had been here, high summer, with a gentle easy sun, the heat not at all oppressive. The air hummed with insect notes, with the sudden chirpings of strong-legged grasshoppers, which stopped as abruptly as they started; high above there was a solitary lark. After the confusion of the cupboard everything seemed as simple, as clear-cut as its song. "I wonder where Penn and Anna are?" Jean asked, but she did not seem alarmed by the lack of an answer. The castle neither welcomed nor threatened them, and they walked towards it between swathes of green bracken, sharp-smelling and full of insect life. Beyond was grass burned pale yellow; it looked silky at a distance but felt prickly and brittle to walk through and to touch.

The path here was so narrow it could only have been made by rabbits. Jean went on ahead of Hugh. But suddenly, as they came round a curve of bracken which had temporarily blocked their view, she stopped dead, gasped and clung to him, her calm not as secure as it had seemed. "Look, *look*," she said.

A little way ahead of them, picking its way across the rough ground, with swaying, jogging quarters, was the horse that Hugh had seen before, and on it the same rider. "It's Penn," Jean said, and the rider turning, Hugh saw that she was right. The red hair was unmistakable. It looked as if he had seen them too because he jerked with his arm, up and forward, then spurred on the horse which moved into a canter, then a gallop. Jean dropped Hugh's arm, stood for a moment, irresolute, touching her brown-stoned brooch. Then she started to run after him, stumbling, once almost falling. She stopped, seeing how hopeless it was, and waited for Hugh to catch up with her.

"It looks as if he's going to the castle too," she said. And then, with a start, "He isn't a baby any more."

"No. He's a man," Hugh said.

They were walking on a paved track now which led straight down towards the castle. There had been an avenue of oak trees along it yesterday and even without them a shadow seemed to fall across Hugh's mind. "Look at the orchards," Jean said. "I've never seen so many apple trees."

Nor indeed had Hugh. Before it had seemed as if the castle had stood on the edges of the world. He could not remember seeing anything beyond it, but did not know which was the truth, that his memory refused to tell him what was there, or that the castle had in reality stood in vacancy, on the brink of a void now quite filled with apple trees laid out in triangular patterns or as vast five-pointed stars. They were above the orchards still as they came down a slope to the castle, so that the patterns were clear, reaching as far as their eyes could see.

They went on downhill. The castle loomed up and soon filled all their vision. Around it was a bank of smooth green turf, and beyond that, from which the castle walls rose direct, a moat full of glassily green water, reflecting turrets and

gates and towers and the grey stone of the walls. Jean saw
Penn on his chestnut horse whose colour almost matched his
own brilliant hair, ride ahead of them across the drawbridge.
The archway beyond gathered him into its shadows, then
hid him entirely. Otherwise there was nothing, no sign, no
sound, not a flicker of life from any opening or battlement,
nor from anywhere. Insects had ceased to sound, the lark – or
any bird – to sing. The seeming lack of life, however, was no
more oppressive than the heat of the sun had seemed. It was
peaceful and comfortable. And again, the silence was not a
negative but a positive force, not muffling sound, but having
a clarity which at once both heightened sense and soothed it,
healing Hugh's anxieties, calming him as a salve might sooth
a wound. The very stones of the castle as they soaked up
light, transmitted calm, and now that Hugh was so much
closer he could see that they were less severely, uncomprom-
isingly grey. He could see green tones and bluish-purple
ones, and even in places a soft pink one, like the tones in bare
flesh.

They stepped on to the smooth green turf. It was not in
fact grass, but some close-cropped, thick and curly plant
which gave beneath their feet like moss and loosed simultaneously a powerful scent.

"It's camomile," said Jean, in an excited voice. "It's
camomile, Hugh, did you realise? I've seen it at Kew. It's
what they've got on Buckingham Palace lawns. It does smell
marvellous." Hugh's mind made a little, sharp, almost
external and totally ridiculous image of a scarlet-coated
guard in a sentry box up against the castle wall. And then
suddenly, as if someone had flicked a switch, he had the same
sense as he had had the last time he remembered coming into
this world; of being in two places at once; of doing two
separate things at once.

He was gliding up a long tunnel underground. He had no
evidence for it being underground, but knew for certain that
it was. There was no sound, not a footfall anywhere. Doors
fell open smoothly to let him pass. The ceilings and walls and
floors were of the same substance, glassy, reflecting, though
reflecting shapes rather than shadows and images, but the
doors that opened to him were at once, and alternately,
opaque and transparent. When his eyes had accepted their
transparency, they would become suddenly opaque, when
his eyes had adjusted to their opaqueness they became again
transparent.

At the same time as this, he was stepping on to the drawbridge and walking across it. He could feel it shake under his
feet, and he had a sense of echo, of hollowness beneath, but
heard the sound within his mind, not actually aloud. In a
moment they had left the drawbridge, had entered the
shadow beneath the archway, then passed out into the light
beyond. The world outside was shut off from them totally, as
abruptly as their own world had been when the cupboard
door had closed. Looking back through the arch, Hugh saw
it as a little bright snapshot, as infinitely remote as a holiday
postcard.

He continued to walk in his glass tunnel. At the same time
this was now his other world, grey walls, grey paving stones,
beneath a sun that shone from a soft blue sky; a benevolent
eye, observing them.

The studs in the huge oak door were like eyes too, as they
had been before. Yet they were more brilliant today than
threatening, multiple brilliancies, each stud reflecting another
little bright sun like the pupil in an eye, and together, he saw
now, forming the same five-pointed star shapes as the apple
trees had. The bird handle of the door stared out from among
them as fiercely as ever. But its eyes went beyond Hugh and

Jean as if the enemy lay elsewhere. The whole effect was of enormous energy and splendour, the more so in their setting, that quiet grey court. Hugh turned the bird head, wrenching it with both his hands; and this time it moved and the door fell open. He felt as if he was being sucked inside by some invisible, inaudible force and pulled Jean with him, after him. The door closed itself behind them.

He could not have said, either then or afterwards, from where his impression of energy, of furious movement came; because everything he saw, that was to be printed indelibly on the eye of his mind for many years to come, appeared as calm as what lay outside.

Till now his walk through the tunnel had coexisted with his journey into the castle. Now his two selves met and fused. He came into this hall from the courtyard of the castle. He also came from his tunnel into the same hall, though he had the impression of being pushed into it from behind, out of the tunnel, while he had seemed to be pulled, sucked in, from the courtyard.

He stood there dazed and momentarily blinded.

The floor and walls and roof of the hall were like those of the tunnel, alternately transparent and opaque. At times Hugh could see through them to the apple trees beyond (which looked, though, insubstantial, vague as a vision or a dream), at times they reflected back everything within the hall. At still other times, however, though they appeared transparent, he could see nothing beyond them but a faint blue haze. The castle might have been drifting in the sky; above, below and all around it, a huge void.

There was an apple tree at the centre of the hall, curiously austere and stern, its leaves and trunk and branches made of a

dim, silverish metal like pewter and its apples of fine gold.
A soft light came from these. It was more like electric than
candle power, in that it seemed less particular to its source
than a candle flame would be, spreading itself further and
more evenly, like light from electric bulbs. Yet it was also
more mobile than electricity; ebbing and flowing within the
fruit and within the hall, as living flames would move.

Beneath the apple tree stood a huge round stone bowl on a
pedestal, a little like a font. Anna was beside it on a raised
platform, and on the step below her Penn, kneeling, his hair
like the golden apples, giving off light or appearing to. They
were Penn and Anna, yet not Penn and Anna. "They're both
grown-up," said Jean in an awed voice, and indeed they
were. They looked exactly as they knew them, but had
greater age and authority, Anna having something of her
mother's brilliance too, although as small and pale as ever.
The brilliance was quieter, dimmer than her mother's; yet
seemed also fuller and more powerful, the difference similar
to that between silver and pewter or silver and iron. She
wore the same clothes as she had worn in their own world,
white skirt, black shirt, sandals, with a medallion on a chain
that Hugh remembered Penn buying her for her birthday,
from the cheap Indian shop in the town. But they might
have been robes on her now, just as Penn's clothes on him
might as well have been armour.

Hugh had recognised them at last, his two kinds of knowledge fusing. Anna was not only Anna but the girl in the
alder grove (he even remembered vividly that the Anna he
knew had a nightdress as red as the dress in the alder grove).
Penn was the man in armour who had passed him, riding,
when he had been rooted, held to the willow tree.

Anna slowly lifted her right hand and held it above the
great stone basin. She moved her hand across the bowl and

back, and where she moved it flames leaped up. The bowl suddenly was full of fire which ran from brim to brim, its light so brilliant that it dimmed the light from the apple tree. The apples grew as pale as stars in daylight.

Nothing in the hall, save for the apple tree, was static, constant now. The fire's continual movement, throwing light upon walls and floor and roof, created lights and shadows which themselves continually changed and shifted, taking on the forms of trees and flowers and of animals and birds. These reflected sometimes out into the sky itself. The sun had gone. The whole sky now was a dark, deep blue. At one moment it seemed full of creatures, leaping, crawling, flying to join the stars. The next, the whole of space appeared to be on fire.

Hugh had to hold tight to his own identity. He felt that if he did not he too would be lost, he too would be shifting shape from second to second. There was a sense in which he actually wanted to lose himself entirely. He might have let go, only something would not allow him to, and that something could only have been Jean. She clung to his hand still, so holding him to himself, to his own form. She chained him, he thought resentfully, but she could not, would not let him go.

Anna and Penn changed form, however. It might have been merely an illusion created by the shifting brilliance of the fire itself, yet at times they appeared indistinguishable from the forms it took. At one moment, Anna became a giantess, her head lost in darkness in the vault of the hall, shadows falling from her outstretched arms across the bodies of Jean and Hugh; her body seeming part of the fire itself. The next moment she had dwindled to her ordinary size. Penn dwindled too. But that was no illusion. Hugh saw suddenly that he had become a baby.

"A baby," he heard Jean say in an awed voice. He was as
if new-born again. Anna bent and picked him up, for a
moment held him close to her. Then she stretched out her
arms and the baby hung above the flames. Hugh knew what
would happen then. But it did not disturb him. He did not
even think it strange, he merely wanted to see what would
come of it.

"Hugh. *Hugh.*" Jean's hand tightened. "She's going to put
him in the fire."

Anna had never appeared smaller or more ordinary. She
was even chewing at her tongue.

"She's going to put him in the fire. She's going to *burn*
him, Hugh," cried Jean. "I'm going . . . I'm going . . ."

"No," said Hugh. "Wait." He did not know what to do.
Without Jean he would not have wanted to do, would not
have done, anything. This, at last, was the decision he had to
make, and he could not make it. Even if his brain had been
working properly his body was rooted, paralysed, just as the
willow tree had paralysed it. And his mind had taken on the
changeability, the volatile nature, of the fire itself. It was
struggling in his head as if with an enemy, changing, changing. Each thought was distinct from the one before it or the
one after, and each thought was only itself, yet seemed to
take on visible form inside his head, forms echoed and
repeated by the fire, the reflections, and the shadows. After
a while he could scarcely tell which were inside his head
and which outside. He only knew that they had come to
threaten him. There were leering demons and dragons,
grotesque creatures, freakish forms, both within him and
without.

He could not connect any one thought to another. His
mind allowed no single logical thread. There were only
two choices and each repeated itself alternately, yet never

connected with an earlier one even though they were the
same. Stop Anna; let her. Save Penn; leave him – these were
the thoughts that went chasing through his head, one after
another, time after time. Allow; do nothing. Allow; do
nothing. Yet each repetition sounded fresh and new, astonishing him. His own consciousness was the single link. His
mind had to make the decision, to snap the succession at one
idea, so inhibiting the next. But even if his mind could have
succeeded in doing that, his body would have been unable to
obey. With an enormous effort of will he managed, fleetingly, to think of Penn, his friend, of his feeling for him, of
his feeling, surprisingly, for Anna too; but it did not help. He
was still powerless.

The thoughts blurred now, increasingly, one losing itself
in another. Hugh felt he was a tree; he felt rooted, fibrous,
with branches; with sap flowing through him, through every
vein. He could feel the whole of himself, both tree and
human, his human body like one drawn by an old-fashioned
anatomist; so that he could feel the paths and strength of each
vein and bone and muscle. He held up his hand and against
the light of the fire it looked transparent. He could see the
glow of the blood, and the bones of his fingers, knobbed
at the knuckles.

"Hugh. Hugh. Oh *Hugh*." Jean was screaming at him
now, was pulling at him, punching him, shaking him as hard
as she could, to no effect. She undid her brooch, the brown
stone in its silver setting, and jabbed its pin into his arm with
all her strength. She was yelling at him at the same time.
Then Hugh yelled too, with pain and fright, and for a
moment, briefly, it cleared his mind. He gathered all his
effort, snapped the succession, stilled the thought he
seemed to need. "Stop Anna," he said slowly, thickly. It was
hardly a decision, more a pressure to which he had at last

acceded. Whether it was what he truly wanted he did not know. His voice could have belonged to someone else. "Stop Anna," it said. "Stop her."

The words, releasing Jean, stilled everything else. Animals, birds, trees, demons, all the actual and illusionary life, vanished or stood still. There was only the swiftness of Jean's movement, so ordinary apparently, so predictable and unexceptional, but which once made suppressed all other movements, all other possibilities. Anna still stood beside the fire, holding the baby over it, but she looked bewildered and small and pale and harmless, a little girl, who let Jean take Penn from her without protest or hindrance. All the energy had gone from her and from the hall. Hugh's mind too was a vacuum. He felt insubstantial, a thin pale shell that would shatter at a touch.

Jean was returning towards him now, holding the baby, followed by Anna walking as if asleep. Hugh waited for them to reach him. Anna moved very awkwardly, and looking at her feet, he saw that a strap on her right sandal had come away from the sole, so that her foot kept on losing it, sliding sideways out of the shoe.

He walked with them now, back the way they had come. The walls were transparent still, but the sky beyond was black and full of white stars. Behind them as Hugh turned to look for the last time, he saw that the fire in the bowl had died. The silvered apple tree was on fire instead, a tree of flame, but a cold, consuming flame, as icy as the stars.

They walked out into a void. It felt like walking off the edge of the world. Hugh expected to find himself falling and for a moment sensed infinite time and distance and, again, infinite possibility, sound growing from him, flowing round him, spreading infinitely, echoing.

The void narrowed and the echo died. The sound

compressed itself, folded itself in, clattered, as if against a closed and wooden wall.

There was a sudden and blinding light. The cupboard doors opened, all four of them walked out on to Hugh's bedroom floor; Hugh, Anna, Jean and lastly Penn in his proper age and size.

The void had gone. Walls had closed round Hugh, confining him, imprisoning him in the narrowest of castles; a castle of bone, he thought. But this castle of bone was himself.

CHAPTER 16

IT was the same but different. They were the same four people but different.

It was Penn who was the hardest to accept. They had known him both as a new-born baby and as a man, and at his present size, much nearer man than baby he still looked surprisingly small. It was like coming into a house you had known as a young child, huge in memory now appearing to have shrunk both in size and in effect. It made Hugh feel diminished – almost cheated too. On the other hand, if he thought of the baby, Penn seemed gigantic; his arms and legs quite grossly thick like trees.

He stood in the middle of Hugh's room now, head down, shaking it, totally bewildered, believing nothing. That was his protection and relief. If he remembered the castle or what had happened he deliberately refused to admit he had. He protested indignantly when they showed him the empty jars of baby food, the bottle with the inch of milk left in the bottom. Indeed, looking at Penn now, Hugh found them quite as astonishing himself. And when they tried to tell him that it was no longer Thursday, that a whole day had passed, he would not accept this at first, merely grew angrier. They had to turn on Radio One (rather a coming and going sound because Hugh's transistor needed batteries) to prove it to him. An excited voice said, "Hullo everyone, *hullo*. It's one o'clock again and welcome to our Friday Show. We've got some great, *great* sounds for you today," – that it was still only one o'clock giving Hugh almost as great a shock as the fact that it was undeniably Friday must have given

147

Penn. While they were in the cupboard no time had passed outside.

They turned off the radio and heard another, though differently excited voice coming from their hall. "Hugh, Jean. *Lunch.* You said five minutes." "Coming," Hugh yelled back, to placate it temporarily.

Penn had to believe this now, that it was Friday; but immediately shut the knowledge out, or rather the fact that it meant anything peculiar. When Anna said "You were a *lovely* baby, Penn," mocking him, and Jean followed in all seriousness, "Oh yes, you were smashing *really*, Penn," he lowered his head again and shook it again violently, as if he was trying to shake something from his eyes.

"Shut up. Shut *up.*" His voice tailed off. Hugh had never seen him less in command of things. That made him feel less safe, less protected too, and again he felt cheated.

He got Anna, alone, into a corner.

"What happened? Did you understand?" he asked. "Why, didn't you?" "I suppose I did," he said. "Glad we got Penn back then?" "Yes . . . aren't you?" "Of course. Or I guess so." There was not doubt exactly in what they said, but a kind of dissociation certainly.

"Does it remind you of anything?" Hugh asked Anna a moment afterwards.

"Does it you?"

"Sort of."

"Well then," Anna said.

"Odysseus," said Hugh.

"Ulysses. What about him?"

"I'm trying to think." Hugh saw Jean across the room, still dazed-looking, yet smiling with relief. By the time he looked back at Anna she had lost interest.

"Oh blast, I've broken my sandal," she said, taking it off to examine it. "Do you think it's mendable?" The strap had parted from the sole itself. Hugh thought it would be difficult. "Well, if it isn't going to be any more use *anyway*," Anna said, and she marched to the cupboard, put the sandal on the shelf and shut the door. The attention of the others centred on to her. They stood and watched in silence, even Penn. Hugh felt properly that he ought to be alarmed but was not alarmed at all, and when Anna pulled open the cupboard door and the sandal lay there unchanged, he knew why, that he had not expected it to change. Penn was smiling now with Jean. He looked more confident already.

"I'm going for a pee," he said, and disappeared downstairs. Jean began putting Hugh's clothes on the cupboard shelves, so Hugh was able to take Anna away again, though she did not seem especially keen to be taken away, staring out of the window for most of the time he was talking to her.

"Odysseus," he said.

"*Ulysses*."

"Oh *stuff* the name. What does it matter?"

"What about him then? *Odysseus*."

"The master told us that in the old religions there was a queen, a goddess, instead of a god. And she had to choose herself a king, a consort."

"Like the Duke of Edinburgh," said Anna, giggling.

"He said that there were a lot of stories about it. Myths. Not just in Greece, everywhere, England even. The point is she always made him immortal, by putting him in a fire or something."

"Like me. Like Penn," said Anna.

"Yes, but there were other ways."

"Ulysses didn't want it; you said."

"He ran away from the goddess woman. Lots of times."

"You stopped Penn," said Anna, balancing on one leg to

149

replace her broken sandal. "Penn didn't run away."

"I know," said Hugh drearily.

"Do you wish you hadn't then?" Anna looked at him sideways.

"What else could I have done?" Hugh said.

As he turned from the window and from Anna, Penn leapt up the stairs noisily, and back into the room. "What are you two gabbing about? Come on, Ann, we ought to be getting home."

"Well, that's it then," Jean said, closing the cupboard door. "You won't have any excuse now, Hugh, not to put your clothes away." At which he felt a surge of mindless, maniacal anger. "Can't you think of anything except tidying?" he bawled at her. It was a relief to feel so angry, yet afterwards again, almost immediately, he felt nothing.

"Hugh, Jean, *lunch!*" Their mother's voice sounded frantic. They went downstairs and Penn took Anna home.

But that was not quite all. In practical terms there was still plenty to be done. Hugh did it with boredom, but glad in a way that his mind was not required. The litter from the baby and from the other transformations of the cupboard had created an extraordinary jumble, which he sorted alone, rejumbled and threw into the dustbins. Jean seemed reluctant to help him. He saw less and less of Penn and Anna now.

For almost the whole of that holiday, things kept on turning up, pieces of stone or metal, dried up pine-needles, wood shavings, other traces of what had passed. He even found eventually, in the pocket of his jeans, the apple he had picked for Jean. It was mummified, quite dry, as if centuries old, and stirred in him a curious and not at all pleasant unease. Everything he found stirred him in some way, gave him pain, a sense of loss; yet it was a fading progression, each time the pain was a little less. He did not like this, tried to reanimate the feeling, but to no avail, logic opposing memory with increasing efficiency. He could not feel the loss of magic because, almost, he did not believe in it any more. Yet in an odd way he was still afraid of it, of magic.

He did not go back to the shop. He avoided even going past it, though his father told him once that it had closed. "I suppose the old boy must have died," he said.

The living evidence remained, of course. The kitten, Humbert, had to go once more through all the processes of growing up, including neutering. He mewed piteously the night he came home from the vet's, as well he might, poor beast, thought Hugh sympathetically; just think of having to have that done to you twice. But nothing now would impede his progression to old age. After a while everyone seemed to forget that he had repeated his beginning.

As for the tortoise Hugh found a box for it to live in and fed it on lettuce and let it out sometimes on the lawn. He became quite fond of it and so did Jean. But after three or four weeks it vanished from the garden, mysteriously, and they never saw it again. "I haven't even got my box," mourned Jean.

Hugh gave his mother the lemon soap, and on that same day, towards the end of the holidays, he was wrapping rubbish in an old copy of the local newspaper when his eye fell on a heading.

PARK PIG MYSTERY

Mr. Frederick Jameson (40) Chief Ranger employed by the Parks Commission was surprised last Sunday to find a large white pig roaming in the park near Fenn lakes. The pig, a sow, and by her appearance recently a mother, had not been reared in the park. To add to the mystery, the mark stamped on the animal's back proved to be that of a farm in North Shropshire no longer in existence.

Neither Mr. Jameson nor other park officials could explain the pig's sudden appearance. Nor has any other explanation been forthcoming. The only clues to the mystery lie in reports of a pig having been seen earlier in Regina Road, passers-by wrongly assuming that the animal had escaped from the park.

"Pigs have not been reared in the park within living memory," stated Mr. Jameson. "We can only assume that someone locally has been keeping a pig in unapproved premises and has not come forward to claim the animal for fear of prosecution. The Police have been informed."